Musician in th

Musician in the Clouds

Ali Bader

Translated from Arabic by Ikram Masmoudi

Georgetown University Press / Washington, DC

The publisher is not responsible for third-party websites or their content. URL links were active at time of publication.

Library of Congress Cataloging-in-Publication Data

Names: Badr, ‘Alī, author. | Masmoudi, Ikram, translator.
Title: Musician in the clouds / Ali Bader ; translated by Ikram Masmoudi.
Other titles: ‘Āzif al-ghuyūm. English
Identifiers: LCCN 2023033352 (print) | LCCN 2023033353 (ebook) |
    ISBN 9781647124434 (paperback) | ISBN 9781647124441 (ebook)
Subjects: LCGFT: Novels.
Classification: LCC PJ7916.A294 A9813 2024 (print) | LCC PJ7916.
    A294 (ebook) | DDC 892.7/37—dc23/eng/20230901
LC record available at https://lccn.loc.gov/2023033352
LC ebook record available at https://lccn.loc.gov/2023033353

∞ This paper meets the requirements of ANSI/NISO Z39.48-1992 (Permanence of Paper).

25 24   9 8 7 6 5 4 3 2 First printing

Printed in the United States of America

Cover design by Martyn Schmoll
Interior design by Paul Hotvedt

Contents

Acknowledgments vii
Introduction ix

Musician in the Clouds 1

Interview with Ali Bader 131
About the Author and Translator 143

Acknowledgments

The translation of this novel was made possible thanks to the encouragement and support of many friends. I thank Ali Bader for giving me the chance to translate his novel and for meeting and interviewing him in Brussels and on Zoom about his ideas and his writing process. I am grateful for the comments and useful suggestions of the peer reviewers, for the support of my family, my friend Ron Martin, the copyeditor, and Ms. Hope LeGro at Georgetown University Press. Special thanks to my colleague and friend Antonio Pacifico for his introductory remarks.

Introduction

Writing about Ali Bader, his personal and professional trajectory, his works, and what these have meant to readers in the Arab world and beyond is never easy. On the contrary, it is a complex activity that requires a thorough approach and attention to the enriching plurality of theoretical perspectives and symbolic values that have characterized his literary production since the beginning.

Bader has always preferred the possibility of making room for new questions and doubts rather than providing his readers with ready-made answers. He has always sought to stimulate their curiosity through a fervent imagination, alongside a solid anchoring in the socio-political reality of our time. Far from (re)producing oversimplified explanations or common representations, he deploys sophisticated strategies that lead his readers to explore their past, present, and future in disenchanted and critical ways. Bader's literary trajectory and works testify to his vast knowledge of the world's intellectual milieu and the main cultural movements that have emerged in Europe and other contexts throughout human history.

One of the most prolific Iraqi writers of all time, Bader has published essays and criticism, as well as journalism; he has also produced several films. He obtained his first success in 2001 with the publication of *Papa Sartre* (*Bābā Sārtr*),

a satirical novel focusing on the Iraqi writers of the 1960s
and their sometimes negative, if not irrelevant, impact on the
cultural production of their time. Through this novel, Bader
proved to be a writer capable of carrying out self-reflexive
practices and one of the finest and most acute chroniclers of
the history of his literary field. *Papa Sartre* also earned him
the appreciation of critics and readers worldwide, in addition to the Iraqi State Award for Literature in 2001 and the
Tunisian Abu al-Qasim al-Shabbi Award in 2003. Among
the works he produced in the early phase of his career, one
should also remember *Shitā' al-'ā'ila* (*The Family's Winter*,
2002), *al-Walīma al-'āriya* (*The Naked Feast*, 2003), and *al-
Ṭarīq ilā tall al-Muṭrān* (*The Road to Bishop's Hill*, 2004).
The latter focuses on the increasing divisions that appeared
in modern and contemporary Iraq during the last century
through the prism of a Chaldean village.

Ṣakhab wa nisā' wa kātib maghmūr (*Clamor, Women, and
an Unknown Writer*, 2005) is another of his most famous
works. In this novel, Bader addresses the material condi-
tions that led to the emergence of his generation of writers,
the novelists of the 1990s, by describing simultaneously
the difficulties that most Iraqi citizens faced under Saddam
Hussein's dictatorship and the harmful effects of the interna-
tional sanctions era.

In 2008, Bader published *The Tobacco Keeper* (*Ḥāris
al-tibġ*), another of his undisputed masterpieces and one of
the most remarkable examples of Arabic musical fiction,
inspired by the writings and thoughts of the tenth-century
Muslim philosopher al-Farabi. This novel inaugurated a new

phase in the author's trajectory, one in which he employed and legitimized the pastiche technique. This phase was also increasingly characterized by crucial questioning of the notions of homeland and nostalgia, identity games, and ever-shifting truths. For example, the existential explorations of the main character of *Mulūk al-rimāl* (*Kings of the Sand*, 2009) revolve around the conflict between the inhabitants of the major Iraqi cities and the bedouins. The insightful reflections contained in *al-Jarīma, al-fann, wa qāmūs Baghdād* (*Crime, Art, and the Dictionary of Baghdad*, 2010) and *Asātidhat al-wahm* (*The Professors of Illusion*, 2011) recall some of the most significant periods of Iraqi history from an artistic and philosophical perspective. Finally, postcolonial concerns and meta-literary preoccupations run through the entire set of works he produced during this phase.

These experiences nourished Bader's subsequent literary activity. Within the texts he wrote in the next phase, Bader showed a keen interest in the themes of travel, migration, and exile, the latter of which generated harsh and fierce debates in Arabic studies and was criticized by Bader himself. After a pause of almost three years, Bader published *al-Kāfira* (*The Sinful Woman*, 2015), a novel that resulted from personal research carried out with migrants who had moved from the Middle East to Europe. Initially conceived as a dramatic text, *al-Kāfira* explores the story of Fatima, a woman who, much like Nabil, the main character of *Musician in the Clouds*, struggles to find her own identity to such an extent that she eventually decides to adopt a Western name.

Musician in the Clouds (*ʿĀzif al-ghuyūm*, 2016) is another result of this long trajectory. It chronologically follows *al-Kāfira* to affirm some of its aesthetic and ethical principles even more convincingly. In this novel, the reader follows Nabil, a young cellist, on his journey from Baghdad to Europe. Inspired by the philosophical and musical thoughts of al-Farabi, Nabil needs to remedy a dissonance—a crucial concept in the writings of the Muslim philosopher—that causes him to be misunderstood by most, and targeted by Islamists. Threatened with physical violence, he decides to leave his country, even though the situation in Europe differs little from the one he experienced in Baghdad. Indeed, in Brussels, Nabil meets not only Fanny, a beautiful and uninhibited girl who frees him from the anxieties that prevented him from being a musician, but also some strange people who police girls' morality and the observance of fasting during Ramadan, and who are convinced of the necessity of destroying all the musical instruments belonging to the "infidels." In other words, it is in Europe, even more than in Baghdad, that Nabil first experiences the sense of loss and disillusionment that characterize each attempt to mix with the "other" or, better, with what lies beyond the "us" in our postcolonial world.

Through Nabil, Bader produces a literary representation of a migrant endowed with agency and in constant search of peace, in contrast to the images of passive or angry individuals that have dominated mainstream media, especially since the outbreak of the so-called "refugee crisis." Not only does Bader counteract images that have come to justify the propaganda of far-right political parties and authoritarian governments during the last decade, but he also questions the romanticized and idealized narratives written by previous generations of Arab writers. In this sense, he carries out a symbolic revolution aimed at subverting some of the strict literary hierarchies and classificatory schemes that weigh on all writers who explore these themes.

By refusing to ascribe to his characters any fixed identity, quality, or status, such as "easterner," "believer," or, more simply, "refugee," Bader opposes the operating principles of these hierarchies, which categorize, classify and order all writers and their literary works according to their personal history or legal status. To put it another way, through an aesthetic that draws on the idea of migrants as individuals characterized by fluid and overlapping identities, Bader aims to avoid any attempt to categorize his work as mere "refugee literature." However, in so doing, he also constructs a parallel world where stories of migrations and diasporas are presented as ordinary processes with their own profound contradictions and ambiguities.

Be it Fatima, Nabil, or even George, the main character of the sequel to *Musician in the Clouds*, entitled *al-Kadhdhābūn yaḥṣulūn ʿalā kulli shayʾ* (*Liars Get Everything*, 2017), we are faced with characters who are the result of mixing, hybridity, and "contamination," precisely like this son of the Iraqi generation of the 1990s or the "generation of the two wars," who has never given up on being "contaminated by" and opening up to the world.

Antonio Pacifico

Université Jean Moulin, Lyon 3

"Give me the waters of Lethe that numb the heart, if they exist, I will still not have the power to forget you."
—Publius Ovidius Naso,
The Poems of Exile: Tristia and the Black Sea Letters

"Everyone must come out of his Exile in his own way."
—Martin Buber

Part One
Where is Exile?

ORESTES: Never shall I see you again.
ELECTRA: Nor will I see myself in your eyes.
ORESTES: This is the last time I will ever speak with you.
ELECTRA: Farewell, my homeland. Farewell.
—Euripides, *Electra*

I

Early in the evening, Nabil got in touch with his father to inform him of his decision to leave the country. He would depart that same night with the help of a smuggler. His father spared no effort discouraging this dangerous idea. He told his son that he would never find happiness in exile. He reminded Nabil of the story of a relative who had lived in America for many years. He had done well for himself, becoming a car dealer at a successful Buick dealership. But after the US occupation of Iraq, and despite the risk, the man returned home. Back in Iraq, he opened a shop that sold Yves Saint Laurent and French perfume—only to shut it down soon thereafter, when he saw that his merchandise did not sell at all after the war. The man tried opening stores in two other places, this time selling luxury handbags by Hermès, Louis Vuitton, Dior, Fendi, Gucci, Prada, Celine, Michael Kors, and other brands that had dominated the world of women's fashion since the nineteenth century. But things did not work out as he had expected. After realizing that people had turned completely away from luxury items, he opened another big store on Karrada Street that sold expensive Iranian prayer rugs.

"Why are you telling me this?" Nabil asked his father.

"Because I think you won't feel at ease there."

"Why do you think that?"

"I know you'll take a huge risk leaving and then you'll get tired and come back."

"That won't happen."

"In the beginning, everyone says the same thing."

"Why?"

"Look, you won't find a good life there."

"How do you know?"

"Everyone who's left has eventually come back."

"They've all come back . . . ha ha ha!" Nabil said dismissively.

After a short silence, his father persevered, speaking in confident tones. "If you're just going to come back like everyone else, why leave in the first place?"

"I won't come back."

"Listen to my advice."

"What's your advice?"

"You won't find the life you dream of away from here!"

"Where do you think I'll find it?" he asked sarcastically. "At home?"

"At least here you know what's going on. You're familiar with the people, their characters, their language, life itself."

"Life?"

"Yes! Life."

"What does life mean to you? I don't find any kind of life here."

"What do you mean you don't find any life here?"

"I can't explain it to you, and I doubt we share the same ideas about life."

"I don't think we'd disagree about the meaning of life."

"We do disagree!"

"What do you mean?"

"I mean . . . "

"Tell me what you mean."

"I don't mean anything! I'm leaving today. That's all!"

♪

Nabil hung up the phone feeling a bit sad. He finished gathering everything he was going to take with him, including his sheet music and two important books—one on harmony and a popular book about the Beatles in relation to postmodern theory.

Nabil's father, who had lived through the golden era of the sixties and seventies, was unable to understand his son's capricious character. However, Nabil's uncle, who had studied in Russia during the heyday of close ties between Iraq and the Soviet Union, understood him better. He was a lively person who liked vodka, smoked cigars, and wore a hat like the one Lenin used to wear. Too bad he'd died two years earlier—right after the Islamist groups took over.

"That was the right thing, too," Nabil thought to himself. His uncle's life of luxury contrasted starkly with the austere tendencies of the Islamist groups, who prohibited all of life's pleasures. *How would he have gotten hold of vodka, cigars, and caviar?*

Even though his uncle had died of cancer, Nabil thought of his death as a kind of protest against the existence of these creatures who wanted to enforce strict Sharia law.

♪

In a small suitcase he gathered all the important things he needed to take with him. It wasn't a lot of stuff anyway; his sheet music had been at the top of the list. Then he lay down on the sofa in his living room waiting for the smuggler to call. A few minutes later he felt hungry. He grabbed some Margherita pizza from the fridge and poured himself a Coke. He put the pizza in the oven, paced around the room, and finally sat down at the table. While the pizza warmed, he thought about what his father had said about the disadvantages of choosing exile and the story of his relative who had returned from America and started warning others against leaving the country to go abroad.

The story reminded him of a parable that the sixteenth-century Persian poet Saib al-Tabrizi had recounted to one of his friends. It was the story of a donkey that was mistreated by his owner, who lived in a village known for its ill treatment and hatred of donkeys. One day the donkey ran away to a neighboring village, where he was astonished to see that they treated donkeys with respect. So he lived there for a long time, enjoying respect and good food, and forgot about all the humiliations he had suffered in his previous village. The time came, however, when he felt overwhelmed with nostalgia for his own village. So, he left. On his way back home, he ran into a fellow donkey from the first village, who seemed terrified and was looking back as he fled.

The returning donkey approached and called out to him, "What are you doing?"

"By God, I have decided to flee this village that humiliates donkeys. I've had enough of this degrading treatment and want to go anywhere else, away from this place."

In a voice full of sadness, the first donkey responded, "Please, listen to me. Go back to your village. You won't feel like a donkey anywhere else!"

II

The oven alarm went off. Nabil removed his pizza from the oven and put it on a plate. The aroma of grilled cheese rose. He put the plate on the table and started eating his pizza while it was hot, without silverware: he liked feeling his hot food with his fingers when he ate.

Soon after eating, he turned on the TV to a porn channel just to kill time as he waited. Porn channels were the only thing available in this country. A store just around the corner sold access codes to any channel for a little bit of extra money. Most of the owner's customers were among the Islamists, one of whom had issued a fatwa that looking at non-Muslim women was acceptable.

With his remote control, Nabil browsed through the porn channels available at that time. He settled on a channel showing sex movies outdoors. He often chose this channel, but this time around the movie was perhaps one of the best ever.

A handsome, dark-skinned man with a light beard and Arab looks—maybe he was Egyptian—with an athletic body, strong muscles, a broad chest and rock-hard thighs. He appeared with a beautiful blond girl, a European for sure. She boasted long legs, big boobs, a slim waist, and a nicely rounded ass. They were swimming in the sea and laughing. The girl started running and laughing. Then she sat down on a chair in the shade of a colorful umbrella. The young man followed her and fell on top of her. He started kissing her neck, running his hands along her thighs and breasts.

Nabil was fascinated by the girl's total surrender as she slowly and leisurely stripped off her underwear. In the background, the beach looked so beautiful, lit by the golden sunrays. It was sex in the open air: on a sandy beach, under a parasol, with a bottle of wine, while the waves quietly died on the sand.

Nabil was completely absorbed by the scene. This was his favorite kind of porn movie. He felt a sense of freedom watching the scene slowly culminating as the girl's wet body shone under the sun. A few grains of sand clung to her reddish-blond pubic hair. He leaned his head forward as if he wanted to get inside the television. He was out of breath, his mouth dry. He observed the man as he encircled his girlfriend's body, adjusting their position to the swelling tune of mysterious music.

Just as the scene was about to end, Nabil's mobile phone rang. It was the smuggler who was waiting for him downstairs.

Now you get here?! Nabil thought, frustrated over missing the end of the scene. Then he assured himself that all porn movies have the same ending. Sex has always had the same movements, the same sounds, and the same ending. What made a difference in this scene was perhaps the place: the sea, the sun, and the freedom of the open air.

III

Nabil felt both excited and ambivalent to be leaving his city. He picked up his suitcase, turned off the television, and turned around to have a last look at his apartment. Then he hurried downstairs. The smuggler's car awaited him at the door. It was an old Honda, perhaps a model from the 1970s. His grandfather used to have a car like that. He had seen it in the family photo album.

He approached the car. It was a blue car that seemed to have been recently repaired on the right side. He took a seat next to the driver.

"Hi," he said without looking at the driver. Then he closed the door. After he fastened his seat belt, he looked ahead, waiting for the driver to hit the road.

"Hi," said the driver, staring at Nabil curiously.

"Haven't I seen you somewhere before?" he asked in a low voice before starting the car.

"I'm not sure," Nabil replied quickly. He turned to the driver and asked, "Where do you live?"

"Here, in the neighborhood."

"So, you must have seen me here."

"Ah, that's right!"

Nabil was used to these kinds of remarks in the neighborhood, like, for example, when a neighbor asked you stupidly, "Where have I seen you before?" and you would answer, "In the neighborhood!" only to hear him say, "Oh! Of course, we're neighbors!"—all the while not feeling stupid at all.

♪

Nabil sat next to the driver. It seemed to him that people only talked for the sake of talking. Someone might ask you a question and not pay any attention to your reply, since they didn't care about what you had to say. Once he had said to his father, "People here want to talk about everything and anything, especially since the war. They just want to chew words. Don't you think so? The art of useless chatter is more common here than it ever was before. It's the only thing people can do and never get tired of doing. They keep repeating things over and over."

His father had laughed. He never took him seriously and always thought his son exaggerated a lot when talking about people or their habits.

"I swear, it's not uncommon to hear people asking you every time they see you, 'Where have I seen you before?' And you tell them, 'Well, I'm your next-door neighbor.' To which they reply, 'Ah, that's true. I remember you telling me that before!' In fact, you've told him a thousand times."

♪

Nabil looked the driver up and down. He looked to be in his sixties, a rural person with gray hair, and a dark black moustache that looked as if it had been touched up with a cheap shoe polish, which was what poor people usually used for dye. He wore cheap made-in-China trousers and a locally made shirt too young for his age. He looked like an Egyptian actor who always played the role of a postman. In vain, Nabil tried to remember his name. Then he decided to just sit and not pay the driver any attention.

As soon as the car set out, Nabil started worrying about whether this man who looked more like a postman than a smuggler was really the person who would get him to Europe, and if he could do that in this old heap that looked like a pizza-delivery car.

He cast a last look at the neighborhood: an overhead power line at the corner, two once-beautiful houses that were now crumbling, and the store belonging to a Christian lady, now shut down after its owner left to join her family in Detroit. As for the building where he lived, it was the only one that was lit, since it had a small generator. The rest of the neighborhood was plunged into darkness due to a power blackout.

IV

Sitting next to the smuggler, Nabil felt happy to leave this neighborhood that had caused him so much humiliation and trouble. He was a cello player. He had specialized in this instrument at the School of Music and Ballet in the al-Mansour neighborhood, and he worked at the National Symphony Orchestra as a classical musician.

It's not easy to be a classical musician in the Middle East. He'd once told his music professor that not only is it difficult, but it's also tragic. It can be both comical and horrible at the same time, like bringing an animal from the North Pole and forcing it to live in an area where the temperature reaches a hundred degrees Fahrenheit in the summer.

In the beginning, he thought it would be easy, that he would be able to figure it out, as it depended on his personal determination and perseverance. He even thought that through this commitment, he might be able to impose what he saw fit on others. He thought that through music he could change things, give meaning to people's trivial lives and transform their emptiness into a luxurious theater or an opulent hotel.

"Don't I have a will?" he once asked his mom as she was knitting him a pullover after he had stopped wearing clothes available in the market—flashy, cheap clothes imported primarily from China and Turkey by stupid merchants whose business had mushroomed after the war.

"Listen," he told her, "I can change my circumstances."

His mother just laughed at him without looking up from her knitting.

"If I gave you this instrument, the sounds would come out strange since you don't know how to play it, but if you trained and practiced, you could extract exquisite meanings from it," he told her.

"People aren't instruments," his mother said, paying no attention to his reaction. He started pacing up and down the room.

Nabil believed that through the power of his will, he could control the musical instrument and change strange sounds into meaningful feelings. He believed that through music he could change the world. He could reach the essence of life and communicate through sounds with people from all walks of life. Through sounds, he could free their souls from their dark sides, reveal hidden meanings, and influence people. This is how he imagined life.

But suddenly he was powerless, unable to replace the old vulgar language with musical strains. Music had no place amidst the clamor and noise of street talk.

"What can I do?" he asked. He put one hand on his forehead and collapsed in desperation on the sofa. As his mother had put it, people weren't machines that he could change and manipulate. Things were more complicated than the theory he had conceived about life and music.

♪

The first opposition Nabil faced came from his neighbors. One day he was taken aback when a group of them gathered in front of the building and asked him to stop annoying them with his music. They couldn't sleep with such idiotic noise.

Nabil was shocked to hear this. There were already numerous sounds one could hear every day in every corner of this miserable neighborhood, although it had been a nice place before the riffraff invaded it after the war. There were cars honking, voices of popular singers coming from devices carried by adolescents roaming the streets, hammers of blacksmiths in the market, cries of peddlers in the streets, sounds of gunshots fired for no reason, and the shrieks of street children. None of this bothered them. The only sound that bothered them was the sound of Nabil's cello when he played Beethoven's "Moonlight Sonata."

"How can I help you?" he asked the group of men and women assembled in front of the gate of the building. They were all talking at the same time.

"How can you help us? We've told you to stop this nonsense that you force us to listen to every day."

"What do you mean?" he pleaded.

"We don't want to hear this disgusting instrument."

The argument was a losing battle, with fifteen people all speaking over one another.

"But this is my profession."

This was the last thread Nabil could cling to in the face of this raving mob.

"It's a filthy profession. Music is forbidden. Haven't you listened to the sheikh at the mosque?"

"Leave me and my God out of this. He knows if it's forbidden or permitted. What do you want from me?"

"You're annoying us. And we don't want you forcing us to hear something forbidden."

"What can I do? Where should I play? In the bathroom?"

"Why not? It's the best place for your shitty instrument," said a bald man who used to be a pickpocket before becoming a man of religion.

♪

Angry and desperate, Nabil went home and closed the door. He tried to sit down, but he was restless and started pacing the room. It was sad to watch the country descending into a frightening chaos. It had started a long time ago. He was silent, but inside he was screaming. His anger was building up like a tree growing where it was not wanted. He didn't know what to say. Inside him, there were many things he couldn't put into words because they were now reserved for the insane and the idiotic. As for artists, they were expected to leave their bodies hung on a peg. He wasn't allowed to object to the youngest idiot in the street, or to disrupt people's lives with elegance and manners.

Nowadays, people hate everything that's beautiful and refined, he thought as he walked down the streets. He felt as if people wanted him to do what they wanted. Even if it was his own skin that itched, he had to scratch it with the nails of the group, with its collusively agreed-upon social codes. As for him and his musical instrument, they were out of place. Everybody wanted him to vanish. Nobody wanted to see him or hear his cello because they thought it would destroy the landscape and break its harmony. The community of the faithful would pray for him to be cured of the disease of music.

Nabil sighed as he sat on the sofa, his forehead resting on his hand. They were the ones who had the power. The ignorant had the power, be it religious, social, or political. And they all wanted to subdue and subject him. Every day they trained him to swallow more stupidities; they trained him relentlessly, and they all wanted him to speak their language.

If only people spoke in the language of music and not with their mouths.

V

Nabil looked out the window as the car left the neighborhood. He felt a growing desire to leave this city where he had lived all his life and where he had his family, his friends, and his first love.

He'd heard enough clichés and tired refrains:

"Oh, I couldn't leave my country. How could I live anywhere else?"

Or, "Despite its many problems, I'd take my country over the biggest paradise on earth!"

It's all bullshit! he said to himself.

In the past, Nabil had been steeped in the idea that he couldn't live without his country. Like all those who had never tried anything else, he used to think that the sky, the air, and the beauty of his city were indisputable. Now, however, he saw that this was a laughable idea, and he had completely abandoned it. He had held many rigid ideas about life, the city, obligations, memories, and the ups and downs of feelings. It was as if the complex world of relationships obeyed the same strict set of laws that made this city so beautiful, and that sea so stunning.

But things had changed. Nabil felt as if a mysterious arrangement was taking him to a distant city, making him change his views about this place where he had lived until now. Life is liable to change, as nothing is stable on this earth. The car had set out now, and there would be no return to this country.

He started counting the many structures that had vanished from his life and those that were threatening to crumble: no more friends, no more bars, and no more beer. As a cello player he had no future in this country. Even his relationship with his parents was just a formality, inessential, lifeless, and empty. It was just rituals. The words that he had to say whenever he saw them were like the words of a hallucinating person, as if he had taken enough drugs to make him talk about family love and true affection.

His relationships were all feigned and inauthentic. They were like a clumsy act in a miserable play, an enactment of a dull text with no resonance—hollow words muttered in the darkness of an empty theater.

He was pleased with this last comparison, and he smiled.

♪

Through the smuggler's car window, he cast a last glance at the neighborhood as he was leaving for good, for the last time. Before it vanished from his sight, he took a deep breath and sighed, "To hell with the rabble!"

Nabil wasn't at peace when he used this expression: *the rabble, the Lumpenproletariat*. He felt resentful and pained. He always used this phrase when expressing his grievances with the world and made clear that Marx had used it in his book *The German Ideology* so that he wouldn't be accused of classist arrogance, even though many intellectuals in

Baghdad didn't shy away from using the word to describe the masses: slum dwellers, the homeless, thieves and gangsters, and all those who had recently invaded high-end residential neighborhoods. Nabil expanded his usage of this phrase to use it satirically. Marx himself had ridiculed the Lumpen-proletariat because of their opportunism and treason during political upheavals. And this was how Nabil saw them too: *They used to be militias working for Saddam. Now they've morphed into religious militias.*

How many times had he suffered the humiliations of the Lumpen! The last time had been the most painful. An Islamist group had attacked him as he was returning home, carrying his cello in its big black case. They had tossed him next to a utility pole on a hot day. He was tired and sweating, trying to make it home as quickly as possible. The leader of the group was their youngest member, with a beardless face. He asked Nabil what he was carrying.

"A cello."

"Ah! What's that?"

"It's a musical instrument."

"Ah, a musical instrument, and a strange one!"

"World music."

"You want to lecture me or what?"

"No, but . . ."

"Don't you know that acting like the infidels is a blasphemy, and that music is forbidden in Islam?"

Before Nabil could say anything, the armed gang hammered his instrument. They broke its strings and slammed it against the ground, kicking it with their feet until they had destroyed it. They were laughing. Nabil looked in silence at the scene before him as neighborhood residents gathered and joined in the laughter with the armed gang. The leader of the group walked up to Nabil. He grabbed him by his necktie and slapped him on the face, making his wire-rimmed glasses fly into the air and land on the sidewalk amid a storm of laughter. Then he slapped him on his other cheek. Nabil wavered and fell to the ground. But as soon as he stood up, the guy grabbed him by his white Ralph Lauren shirt, which Nabil liked a lot, and started tearing it with rage as if he hated this kind of shirt or the color white. The whole neighborhood laughed hysterically.

♪

Nabil felt a deep humiliation and went up to his apartment, breathing heavily. He headed to the fridge, grabbed a cool bottle of water, and drank the whole thing. He looked in the mirror and inspected his bruised face. He removed his torn shirt and threw it on a chair, then went to the window to take a look at his instrument. It had been reduced to scattered pieces in the hands of children, who were running around laughing and trying to play it.

He sat down on the sofa.

How was he supposed to walk down the street again after the humiliation he had suffered?

In the past, he had been disliked in the neighborhood, but he had been respected; everybody knew who he was and respected him. He was a quiet person, wearing prescription glasses—a sign of his intelligence—well dressed and elegant, with a face that was hard to read. He hadn't looked like the masses in the street. He carried a strange musical instrument and walked straight and with determination. His daily schedule had been clear: every day he left home in the morning and came back in the evening.

In that moment, he wondered: how would people look at him? How would he look them in the eye after the slaps and humiliation he had suffered, the destruction of his instrument, and the blow to his self-esteem? What had happened to him that day was horrible. He felt completely crushed, and his humanity was totally erased as if they had transformed him from a human being into a mop rag.

This incident reminded him of what had happened once to one of his elementary school teachers. Professor Jamal was a dignified person, tall, silent, and always well-dressed and elegant. He usually wore a hat and carried a leather satchel. When he walked in, all the students fell silent. He was by far the most respected of all the teachers because of his dignified persona. One day he walked across the street from the school, just when all the students had been let out. They stopped in front of the big gate, and at that moment a ferocious dog singled him out and attacked him. The teacher screamed at the top of his lungs and started running away, with the dog hot on his heels. His hat flew into the air, and out of fear he let go of his satchel while a storm of satanic laughter seized all the kids. Because of this scene, the professor lost all his dignity and prestige. Nobody respected him anymore, and after this, students started rebelling against him and mocking him.

Nabil wondered how he was going to walk down the street

again after his humiliation. How could he look people in the eye? And how were they going to look at him?

He turned the TV on to a porn channel and stretched out on the sofa.

♪

The next day he couldn't focus his attention on anything. He was scattered. In the morning, his ideas were foggy, and his body was tired. He was confused, as though he were hallucinating. He didn't know what to do or how to regain his inner peace. He felt more angry than sad and more tense than depressed. He didn't pity himself. He was just extremely angry.

Feeling clueless and powerless, he started letting out strange cries while he was still in bed, closing his fist tightly, then releasing it, cursing, and uttering repeated and stupid insults, which made him angry with himself. He wanted to come up with a new language for himself so that he could insult his tormenters in all languages, including languages he didn't know: "Fuck off, *merde*, *fils de putain* . . . ," but this was all in vain.

What could he do?

He was losing it. He was losing his mind.

Music is the queen of all things, he thought to himself. Through its sounds, he could name anything that came to his mind. Through its harmony, he could dive into the surrounding daily life, delve to the bottom of it, and explore its depths. There was nothing he couldn't name or identify through music. But with the Arabic that he spoke so fluently, he felt completely unable to understand the many things that had begun multiplying in the surrounding chaos, because he couldn't find the right words to refer to them.

He fell silent. Lying in bed, he grew still. He felt paralyzed. After his humiliation, he felt unable to respond. Everything around him had lost its meaning. The world was dumb, without intelligence, without imagination. It was incomprehensible to him. He didn't want to name or embrace it. He couldn't tell the difference anymore between a living being and an inanimate object! An animal and a stone!

Since he hadn't been able to respond to the mob the night before—worse still, he hadn't even been able to confront them—he felt entitled to respond to them while lying in bed.

♪

Nabil remained in bed until morning without even thinking about anything. Little by little, he regained his ability to put thoughts together. But thinking about the issue plunged him into a strange sadness, and he didn't like to lie in bed sad and depressed.

He asked himself, *What to do now, here in bed?* The only way to recover his dignity was to humiliate them in his imagination. He invoked the scene one more time in his mind, but he imagined it differently. Instead of them hitting and humiliating him, he attacked and humiliated them.

He imagined an incredible natural strength within him, though he didn't know where it came from. When they moved against him, he didn't tremble with fear, but they did. He advanced toward them perfectly quietly and calmly. After the first strike, they became like limp rags in his hands.

They were shaking before him. He confiscated their weapons and destroyed them before throwing them to the ground. The children picked up their pieces as they had with the remnants of his instrument, and ran off to play with them. He even tore their clothes as they had torn his Ralph Lauren shirt. After that, he slapped them repeatedly, and none of them was able to return the slaps. They begged him for mercy as the people in the neighborhood laughed and mocked them.

♪

He got out of bed feeling happy. Hitting them and taking revenge in his imagination had somehow appeased and pacified him, producing a state of temporary amnesia regarding what had happened to him the night before.

He hurriedly put on his clothes. But when he was about to leave the house, he hesitated. He didn't want to bump into anyone from the neighborhood. He was ashamed of what had happened to him with the gang.

He peered over the balcony. The street looked empty. He left quickly, without running into anyone. On his way back, at noon, he came face-to-face with the same armed Islamist group. He was uncertain how to proceed. As he approached, the leader of the gang smiled at him and asked him politely to stop. Nabil stopped, his heart racing. The leader asked him, "You're the guy we disciplined yesterday, aren't you?"

". . ."

"What's wrong? Why don't you say anything?" said the gang leader, as he swaggered back and forth in front of him. "Are you dumb?"

Nabil was shaking. He replied softly, "What do you want me to say?"

"Say anything you like."

"Nothing . . . I have nothing to say."

"We can't let you go without your saying something."

The armed guys surrounding him were seized by laughter. There were five of them, all in their twenties, dressed strangely, like the characters in religious TV dramas portraying Muslims fourteen hundred years ago. They had long beards, and each of them carried a Kalashnikov. Next to them there was a modern four-wheel drive Toyota.

"Are we bothering you?" asked the leader of the group.

"No, not at all . . . On the contrary."

"So, you're not upset with us?"

"No. Why would I be?" Nabil asked, looking uneasy.

"What we did yesterday was for your own good. We saved you from God's wrath."

"Thank you. Now let me go home."

"We will. But we have something else to bring up with you first."

"What's that?" Nabil asked with surprise.

"Listen, we've forgiven you for your violation of Islamic rules."

"I thank you for that."

"You should understand that music is a sin. We forgave you in the past because you were ignorant. We disciplined and educated you, and now you'll have to make expiation so that God can forgive you. You'll have to pay a certain amount of money to help build a mosque in the neighborhood."

He continued, "As you know, most of the people in this neighborhood used to be wealthy. Yet they never built a single mosque here. Thank God we got rid of them. The new residents want to build a mosque, and we're now collecting donations. You need to make a contribution. What do you say?"

"Can you give me some time to think?"

"Think about what?"

"About this question."

"What question?"

"The question about the mosque."

"Does that require thinking?"

 "I just need time to see . . ."

"To see what?"

"To see whether I can make a donation or not."

"Whether you'll donate or not?"

"I didn't mean I wouldn't make a donation. Why are you so edgy?"

"You're getting on my nerves. Do you think building a mosque is a bad thing?"

"No, I swear, that's not what I said, but . . ."

"But what?"

"Don't I have the right to think?"

"You can think when the question has to do with something that might be bad, but not when it involves good."

"I just wanted to think."

"The mosque involves good, but you want to think. This means you are either against doing good, or against God."

"No, that's not true."

"Then it means you're an atheist, or a secular person."

"No, no, not true."

"So why do you need to think?"

"I just wanted to see how I can come up with the money for you."

The leader of the group smiled and said to him, "Ah, OK, that's good. This means that in principle, you're not against the idea, right?"

"No, no, not in principle."

"That's good," said the leader as he looked at the group, who were smiling.

"Can I go now?"

"Why are you always in a hurry?"

"I need to go start thinking about how I can come up with the money . . ."

"How much time do you need?"

"Give me just a couple of days."

The leader of the gang smiled, and so did the other gang members. They relaxed their grips on their weapons.

"We'll give you a week. Is that enough?"

"Yes, that's quite enough."

"So that they can't say we're extremists and aren't tolerant with people."

"You're very tolerant."

"Some people accuse us of being extremists. We could have killed you yesterday because you violated the rules of Islam, and we could have come to your house right now and taken all your money. Instead, we've given you a week to make a donation to help build the mosque."

"That's good."

"We also helped you before God. This way, He'll forgive your heinous deed of playing music instead of praying and remembering Him."

"That's also good."

"Yet the fools still call us extremists. Despite all our leniency, they still call us extremists. These infidels who imitate Westerners and Crusaders call us extremists!"

"That's terrible."

"May God curse them."

"Yes."

"Well, go home now, and we'll come and see you in a week. If you don't have the money, you'll have to buy your shroud!"

"OK, thanks for the advice."

VI

As soon as he heard what the gang leader said, Nabil hurried to his apartment. He went up the stairs, opened the door, and rushed in. He paused a moment and thought. What was he going to do? He had no clue, and his head was empty. He had been terrified when the leader of the armed group talked to him, and he had lost his nerve. The leader had been getting very serious and tense as he talked to him, and his men had gripped their weapons tightly.

Nabil stood confused in the middle of the room. He could hear them in the streets as they jumped into their cars and closed the doors. A few minutes later he heard their tires squealing against the asphalt as they left the neighborhood.

♪

First, he sat on the sofa, but he was too tense to sit and relax. He got up. He couldn't think properly. His mind was blank, and he felt hungry. He headed for the fridge. He found a piece of fried steak left over from the day before. He should have warmed it up, but he abandoned that idea. He was too nervous. He took a piece of brown bread from a wooden box covered with a white tissue and looked for beer in the pantry. There was none. The carton was empty. He looked in the fridge and found one. It was the last beer he had. If he drank it, there wouldn't be another.

He started eating the cold steak with the brown bread, and

sipping the beer. If the armed gang or anyone else had asked him to build a bar, he would have offered them all the money he had without question. But for a mosque, the issue needed some thought. All the terrorists came out of mosques. Not a single terrorist came out of a bar to blow himself up. If they had told him they intended to build a bar where the youth of the neighborhood could sit, chat, and have a good time together and not think about killing themselves or others, he would have gladly responded to this, but building a mosque—that wasn't so easy to accept.

Then he mused that drinking wine wasn't forbidden in the Islamic tradition. Throughout history, Muslims have always had wine. Even Abu Hanifa al-Nuʿman, the great Muslim jurist who lived in Baghdad in the eighth century, allowed drinking and selling wine. He distinguished between drinking and getting intoxicated. Only losing control of one's mind was a sin. So one can drink as long as one doesn't get intoxicated. Abu Hanifa even permitted drinking wine and beer, but Nabil didn't know what his position would be on whiskey, mojitos, and Campari. As a modern Scottish invention, whiskey wasn't around in the time of Abu Hanifa, but Nabil's imagination always clung to the idea of a certain eighth-century Baghdadi poet who worshipped wine. His name was Abu Nuwas. Nabil imagined him sitting at a bar holding a glass of Johnny Walker on the rocks, his father's favorite brand.

After finishing the steak, the brown bread and the small can of beer, he felt the urge for a second beer. But how could he get one? Wasn't there a solution to his problems? The humiliation he had suffered, the blow to his pride, the music he'd had to abandon—was this a life? What was he going to do?

For a long time, he had thought about fleeing to Europe, but it had never been the right time. Now it was long overdue. Here he was, sitting next to the smuggler who was going to take him to the place he dreamed about, to a life beyond the ocean wide. He recalled a couple of verses of poetry about this, but he couldn't remember the poet's name:

We'll go over there
We'll go to a Utopian City
A city beyond the ocean wide,
Where the artist lives like a Musician in the Clouds.

Nabil wondered, *Is it possible to get to the Utopian City, to life beyond the ocean wide, which some poets call "the other place," with a vehicle that looks like a pizza-delivery car and a smuggler who looks like a mailman?*

VII

The blue Honda came to a full stop in a remote location that looked like the desert. Nabil didn't know where he was. He had never been here before.

"Where are we?"

The smuggler didn't answer his question. He looked worried as he tried without success to make a phone call. The road was unpaved, with desert vegetation scattered here and there. It was getting dark, and the air was growing steadily cooler. Nabil guessed that they were close to the Turkish border and that the real journey was now imminent. It could hardly have begun with the blue Honda and the guy who looked like a mailman.

It didn't make sense to go to Europe in this kind of car, with a driver with this appearance and a face devoid of any sign of intelligence.

Was Nabil right to be concerned about the means of travel, such as the car's model and the smuggler's looks? He might have been overly concerned with these details at that moment. But his worries seemed justified because he was afraid he had been duped. It happened so frequently these days.

♪

Nabil spent more than fifteen minutes observing the driver, who was trying desperately to contact his friend. Then he ended the call and looked at Nabil with a worrisome uncertainty in his eyes. Just before he said a word, though, he received a phone call from the person he was trying to call. At that moment, the driver's tone changed, and he looked more confident. Nabil felt reassured and broke into a grin when he heard the driver talking to the person he needed, explaining their whereabouts. After the call, he said to Nabil with a smile, "We're safe. The smuggler is on his way. He will lead you to Turkey."

"So, you're not the smuggler?"

"No, I'm a taxi driver taking you to the border. I don't have to worry about the rest."

"The smuggler is on his way?"

"Yes! He'll be here in thirty minutes tops."

The driver stuck his phone in one pocket and took his keys out of the other. Then he turned and headed for the car.

"Where are you going?"

"I'm leaving. You just wait here; the smuggler will be with you shortly."

"Are you kidding me? You won't move from here until someone shows up to take me."

"That's none of my concern."

"What do you mean, man? Are you crazy or what? Did you just bring me here for a pleasure outing?"

"The smuggler only paid me to bring you to this place."

"What place? Do you know this place? Where do the cars come from, and where do they go from here?"

"I don't know. I just followed the directions the smuggler gave me."

"Please! Don't leave before he comes."

Nabil grabbed the driver's hand so tightly that he knew he wouldn't let him go no matter what. The driver huffed angrily and said, "If you weren't my neighbor, I would have left you here, but since we're neighbors, I'll wait until the smuggler shows up and takes you."

The Honda driver took a cigarette out of the pack and started smoking irritably while Nabil, apprehensive and suspicious, stood staring into the darkness as he waited for the smuggler to show up. To avoid changing his mind, Nabil recalled everything that had pushed him to leave this country. He remembered a few days before, one of his friends making a good diagnosis of the situation as little by little things were falling apart.

"What a precise analysis," Nabil had told him.

But what really pushed Nabil to leave the country as soon as possible was music. In his opinion, life had no meaning without music. He had said just this to a fat friend of his, who sat facing him wearing a beautiful French necktie, more like a blue foulard, with fine white dots, not tied into a knot around the neck but held by a golden ring.

"Imagine if we had to throw away all these things and couldn't wear them anymore. We would wear a *dishdasha* and sandals and wrap our heads in rags so that we could blend in."

Nabil cared less about what he wore than about what he did, and specifically, about playing music. Unlike most of his friends, this was what really mattered to him in those days.

"Do you think they'll let you play the cello?" his friend had asked him.

Nabil looked worried. He knew that in this country there were two antagonistic cultures: a culture of the arts, which had begun to disintegrate with Saddam's wars, and a rising populist culture based on the revival of violence and bloodshed replacing the violent state that had collapsed.

Where did he fit in this fight?

Nothing would solve this dilemma but fleeing to "a life beyond the ocean wide," an expression he preferred over *migration*, *refuge*, and *exile*.

At long last, the other smuggler showed up in a big pickup.

VIII

Nabil's worries hadn't dissipated yet. He had heard plenty of stories about smugglers. The stories varied, but they all ended the same: with horror, inspiring fear. It wasn't just about deception and fraud or other familiar tricks. There were worse things, such as theft, kidnapping, and even rape and murder. The most common thing, however, was deceit. You put all your money in the pocket of a smuggler only to find yourself back to square one, back to where you had come from, in a condition worse than when you left. But Nabil had always found excuses whenever he listened to one of these stories. He would say, "It will be different with me."

When he decided to leave for Europe, Nabil picked the easiest but most expensive route. He didn't want to cross in a rubber dinghy from Izmir to Greece: the dinghy could capsize, and he would become food for the fish. The mere thought made him tremble. Instead, he took the advice of one of his relatives, who suggested that he travel in a pickup truck to Turkey and from there to Europe: no border crossing, no coast guards, and no drama.

"A VIP refugee!" his relative had said.

♪

He climbed into the pickup, which took him from that remote place in the direction of Europe. He was cautious and suspicious as he sat next to the Turkish driver, who only spoke a few words of English. His beard was a bit long, and he had narrow set eyes. He didn't look like a dangerous person or a criminal, but looks can be deceiving.

By the break of dawn, the journey had started to feel more pleasant. They were driving through Turkish cities with beautiful buildings, wide streets, boutiques, huge supermarkets, beautiful tourist attractions, and natural landscapes. Nabil's mood was improving, and he started chatting with the driver, using sign language and a few English words. He smoked with him and shared an orange.

At the beginning of the journey, Nabil thought he would arrive in Belgium in this pickup. He would get there just by sitting next to the driver, while they smoked cigarettes and ate oranges. But then the driver surprised him by telling him that he would only take him to the European border. From there, Nabil would have to cross through Europe to get to the other side, where Belgium was located.

The money was supposed to have been paid in full to the smuggler via a third party. But the smuggler insisted that he needed an extra two hundred dollars from Nabil, especially after he saw how well dressed he was. Nabil looked elegant, dressed more like he was going on a date than fleeing to Europe as a miserable refugee.

♪

No sooner had he crossed the border than he climbed, with the help of the smugglers, into a big truck with twenty other young men. This is how his first anxiety at the sight of the pizza-delivery car that took him to the Turkish border ended.

Then came the joy of traveling in the pickup truck, cross-ing through Turkey, smoking and munching on oranges and pistachios only to find himself in another truck, which was supposed to get him to his final destination.

It was a closed truck, used for tire exports. Nabil had paid seven thousand dollars to a smuggler just so that he could be placed in a big wooden box with little openings for air. There was bottled water, canned food, and plastic bags to be used for pooping and peeing. It was going to be a ten-day journey to the Utopian City. The truck traveled by night and stopped during the day so that the driver could sleep. Whenever they stopped and before they set out at night, the driver would collect the plastic bags and throw them in a remote place.

This is how Nabil traveled, counting the hours inside a wooden box in a closed truck. He couldn't see the road, and he didn't know how they made their way or where they were. He only knew the vehicle was moving with him in a box. What worried him was the thought that the smugglers might dupe him.

What if there was no journey to Europe? he thought to himself as he tried to forget the uncomfortable situation he had put himself in. *What if this was nothing but a scam?* Similar stories had circulated amongst immigrants who had tried to get to Europe at any price.

Scratching his head, Nabil thought to himself, *It's so com-mon for something like this to happen these days. It's not at all difficult to imagine.* The pickup he had climbed into could have roamed the streets of the same town without taking him anywhere, going in circles the whole night. He had heard so many stories about smugglers and their scams. It was always done in the same way. You would be inside, not able to see anything, thinking that you were on the right track and that the smuggler was taking you where you had dreamed of going.

IX

The only time Nabil got out of the truck on the way was when he and an Afghani youth ran out of the plastic bags they used for bodily wastes. They talked to the driver and asked him to stop for them. Grumbling angrily, the driver agreed to get them close to a forest where they could relieve themselves. The Afghani guy went first. When he returned, he said to Nabil, "I think we're in Poland."

Then it was Nabil's turn to leave the truck and make his way to the dark forest. He didn't know how the Afghani gathered that they were in Poland, as it just looked like any woods in Turkey. But the word *Poland* struck a chord with Nabil like a magic wand. As soon as he heard it, he was transported back to his childhood in the 1980s, at which time his uncle had had a Polish girlfriend named Anna. She would come from Warsaw to Baghdad to visit him. His uncle invited him to accompany him and Anna and one of her girlfriends—Eva, who worked at the Polish Embassy in Baghdad—to a party at the luxurious Hotel al-Rasheed in Baghdad. The three of them started drinking vodka and dancing to loud music under the strobe lights. Not only did the uncle drink and dance with Anna and her friend, but Nabil saw him reach out and fondle her between her thighs. She was a light-skinned blond girl. Never had Nabil seen such a light-skinned woman, still less a woman's thighs.

Then they went to a sumptuous house in the neighborhood of Arsat al-Hindiyya, an upscale quarter built in 1917
during the British occupation of Baghdad. The house had a
luxurious garden and a swimming pool, and there were many
guests, among them foreign youths who worked with diplo-
matic delegations and companies during that time.

Nabil started observing the girl as she sat next to his uncle. Her face was glowing as they exchanged whispers. From
time to time, his uncle would caress her face or her arms. She
smiled and continued chatting with him, her wide, dark eyes
tender and affectionate. Then the two started humming an
English song and cuddled and laughed. Then Anna walked
toward the window and stood looking at the street as the early
winter night descended on Baghdad. His uncle followed her
and flirted with her in public. Two minutes later, after Nabil
went inside the large hall to put his plate on the table, he saw
Anna in his uncle's arms, absorbed in a long fervent kiss, her
eyes shut and her face aglow. She slowly withdrew from his
uncle, who looked intoxicated. Out of the corner of her eye
she looked at Nabil, who sat observing them in wordless embarrassment. She stopped and wrapped her arms around her
boyfriend as he embraced her with a kind of uninhibited joy.
Then he laughed out loud, his face enlivened by an affection
Nabil had never seen before, which aroused his jealousy and
curiosity at the same time.

♪

Nabil would never forget how, after his uncle went to the
bathroom, Anna came over and talked to him. "You had a

good time, right? I was looking at you. I saw you watching me."

"No, I wasn't," he answered and lowered his head in embarrassment.

She hugged him and tousled his hair, laughing like a little girl.

"Did you see me flirting with your uncle? Were you jealous? Did I laugh more than I should? Do you think I'm cute?"

Nabil didn't answer her questions. But when she hugged him, her body infused with the fragrance of soap, he closed his eyes tight and almost fainted.

♪

Nabil didn't remember whether it was his uncle who invited him to the party or if the family had asked him to accompany his uncle so that he could keep an eye on him, lest the Polish girl seduce him and corrupt his morals.

When he returned home, he didn't tell his family what he had seen. The family asked him about the party. They wanted to know what had happened, but he didn't say a word. His mother asked him, "Did you like the party?"

"No," he answered mischievously.

"Why?"

"It was boring, and I didn't like the people. Nobody talked, and no one danced."

His uncle repressed a smile, but his face was still glowing with love.

Nabil felt he had had a great time indeed. For the first time in his life, he had enjoyed seeing two lovers flirting together at a wild party. His uncle told him that in Europe you could see people flirting everywhere and it was no big deal. Perhaps one of the things that motivated Nabil to undertake this dangerous journey was the curiosity to experience this feeling: to flirt publicly in the street, in front of everyone, without fear, and to kiss someone in the open. In any case, this memory made him happy and excited for a long time. He always remembered this girl and the lasting effect she had had on him.

However, one scene from his childhood had kept coming back to him: his uncle had stripped the Polish girl naked except for a necklace she was wearing. He had stretched her out on the sofa and made love to her. Nabil couldn't tell whether this scene had really taken place or was merely a product of his imagination. In any case, the word *Poland* became like a magic wand for Nabil. It evoked the same image every time he heard it. As soon as he got back to the truck and groped for his seat in the darkness, he felt an erection and fell asleep without knowing how.

X

The smuggler looked around as if he were searching for somebody. Then he said to Nabil in a low voice, "Get out quickly. This is Brussels."

"Brussels . . . Right. Brussels?! Really??!"

"Hurry up, man!"

At first Nabil couldn't believe it. As soon as he got out of the vehicle, he saw an unlit, dirty square that could have been any square in the Third World. He got out slowly, dragging his bag behind him. He looked at the place in disbelief, and his jaw dropped. He looked right and left and asked himself, *Is the smuggler trying to trick me?*

The smuggler, hurried and scared, dragged him by his hand and pulled him along. They crossed the street toward an old house on the corner of a large, dingy square, on another corner of which there was a laundry mat. The smuggler whispered gruffly, "Hurry, hurry up!"

Nabil followed, dragging his suitcase, but he lost his shoe on the way. He withdrew his hand from the smuggler's, turning and yelping, "My shoe, my shoe!"

"Is this really the time? The police might see us."

"Yes, but I don't have any other shoes."

The smuggler opened the door with a key and rushed him inside.

"Are we in Brussels?" Nabil asked the smuggler in disbelief.

"Yes, this is Brussels. Are you drunk or what?"

"No, but it's dirtier than Baghdad."

"This neighborhood's full of Muslims, Turks and Moroccans . . ."

"Oh, I see!"

The smuggler accompanied him inside. The staircase was filthy, and the smell of old shoes and socks hung in the air. The trashcan was full, with garbage and unknown items piled around it: old books without covers and cardboard boxes near the stairs, two old bikes stationed near the door, and a broken mailbox, with letters scattered around it. The place looked like a dovecote on a roof that had not been cleaned for months.

The smuggler climbed some shaky wooden stairs with Nabil, leading him to a small apartment. He turned on the light, handed him a key, and said, "Listen, this is temporary. Don't forget that. Don't be stupid like the guy who came before you: he stayed here a month but didn't turn himself over to the police. Hide here a day or two, then turn yourself over to the police as a refugee. The rent is paid for a full month, but that won't do you any good. You have to go to the camp in order for them to recognize you as a refugee."

"And what if they don't recognize me as a refugee?"

"You go back to Iraq, and we'll bring you back here under another name."

"Oh, okay!"

"Don't worry. There's a solution to everything, but it comes with a price."

"I understand."

♪

Nabil threw his suitcase on the sofa in the living room. Then he looked around the apartment. It was in total chaos, like the aftermath of the battle in the Persian War described by Gobineau in the nineteenth century. A disproportionately large armoire occupied almost all the space. Aside from the broken chairs and dirty area rug, a cheap poster covered the wall. There were also two flags: Turkish and Moroccan. No sign of the Belgian flag. A small hallway led to a kitchen that looked more like a crowded chicken coop, with a two-burner portable stove on a table, and dirty pots and pans piled on top of each other. The place reeked and oil spots covered the walls.

Is this possible? Am I in Belgium?

Then there was the bathroom, which was very small, with a rusty shower and a pale yellow light, just like the one in the vegetable store in his neighborhood in Baghdad. And it was anything but clean. More surprisingly, instead of the toilet paper that Europeans use, there was a spray device like the ones they generally use in Muslim countries.

Is this possible? Am I in Brussels?

♪

Nabil's idea of Europe was very different from what he saw now before his eyes. His image of life in Europe was excessively idealistic: luxury living, five-star comfort, shiny floors, places exuding perfume—not this miserable ruin, which wouldn't even count as an apartment back home. His own apartment in Baghdad had been better than this.

He felt dizzy and feverish. The idea that those smuggler thieves roamed the same place and dropped migrants in a yard or a house in a neighborhood of Istanbul, Izmir, or Adana buzzed in his head like the droning of a bee.

Nabil was dumbfounded; he flung himself onto the sofa and reached for the remote control next to him. He turned and saw a television mounted on the wall. He flipped calmly through the channels. Most of them were Turkish or Moroccan; a few were Western with advertisements; but most were sports, news, music, fashion, cooking, and contests. To his surprise, there were no porn channels. *Is it possible that there are no porn channels in Belgium? Do they apply Sharia law here?*

Soon he felt hungry. He went to the fridge and found a sandwich wrapped in a bag with "Mohammad's Snack" written on it in Arabic. He devoured the sandwich and then went to the bathroom. When he came out, he felt exhausted, so he stretched out on the sofa and fell into a deep sleep. At midnight he woke up tired and thirsty. He drank a glass of water and grabbed the remote control. In vain, he surfed the channels, looking for porn. He settled for a music channel. The music was very romantic and dreamy. Listening attentively, he felt at peace with himself.

Suddenly the image of al-Farabi, the eighth-century Arab philosopher, popped into his head. Al-Farabi had viewed music as a key element of the Utopian City because for him, the idea of justice derived from musical harmony. Could we consider the idea of happiness a mathematical or logical equation? Al-Farabi says yes, but the rabble says no.

Nabil smiled. Was he going to use the expression "the rabble" in Europe too?

He turned over, shut his eyes, and listened intently to the peaceful music coming from the television. He was still thinking about al-Farabi's ideas of using music to treat psychological and nervous illnesses. He felt happy, or at least at peace. Music is magic—almost hypnotism.

XI

A few minutes later, Nabil sat upright on the sofa and placed his hand on his cheek, with al-Farabi still in his head. *Was al-Farabi smarter than the Greek philosophers when he went beyond their formalist ideas about music?* Nabil wondered. The Greeks understood music simply as sound in motion, but al-Farabi deepened his understanding to identify emotions in music. Nabil felt peaceful and relaxed, as if he were floating through the clouds. At that moment, he heard a faint voice which quickly grew louder. It was a Muslim praying out loud. The same words came again and again, like a phrase repeated over and over in Oriental music.

He remembered his grandfather praying out loud like that, especially in the morning. It had prevented Nabil from sleeping. His grandfather had had an ugly voice, just like the voice coming from the neighboring apartment, but he had never lowered it while at prayer. It would have been different if his voice had been beautiful, but it was hard to bear, repeating the same things endlessly.

But there was something else.

Are we in Belgium? At that moment, he felt that the idea of al-Farabi had crumbled in his mind. The ideas of music, justice, and happiness gradually vanished as he was over-taken by the fear that he might not be in Belgium. *Where am I, really?*

At first, he denied the reality of what he had just heard. He tried to question it, but then it was confirmed. The voice was clear, and the words were enunciated distinctly in the next room. Feeling desperate and sad, he threw his body on the sofa. This voice had eroded the little hope he had. He felt sad and anxious that he might not be in Belgium, but in some country that bordered on his, like Turkey or Iran. Smugglers were thieves. Their stories were always the same. Unable to fall asleep, he tossed and turned. He put the pillow over his ears for a few minutes and felt peaceful. The only thing that was amusing or enjoyable to him amid this depressing atmosphere was the memory of the Polish girl and how his uncle had slept with her on the sofa while he looked on as a boy. Her soft, white legs were imprinted on his mind.

XII

Nabil got up early in the morning. He opened his suitcase and unpacked his clothes. *I forgot the towel.* He realized that it wasn't just the towel he had forgotten. When he traveled, he always forgot many things. He had packed just the minimum. However, he had guessed that when he arrived in the Utopian City, he would at least need some new clothes, so he had brought some with him.

Oh shit, I also forgot my second pair of jeans.

He put on a new shirt but kept on the pants he had traveled in. He rinsed his face and brushed his teeth, then applied some oil to his hair and combed it. He looked at his moustache. He didn't know if he should shave it off, or keep it. Having asked himself this question many times in Baghdad, he had postponed the decision for Europe. However, he wasn't sure whether he was actually in Europe now. He put on his shoes, fastened his belt, and descended the dirty staircase.

As soon as he saw the street, his anxiety was dispelled. He wasn't in Turkey, Iraq, or Iran. He was in a city that he couldn't identify clearly at first glance. However, it was undoubtedly in Europe. It was most likely a neighborhood for immigrants. There were many black people walking in the streets, as well as Arabs, Asians, and Latins. He saw many veiled women, but there were European women as well.

A blue sign on the wall indicated that it was Rue Sergent De Bruyne in Brussels' Anderlecht neighborhood. The sign read that this sergeant had died in the year 1812 as he was establishing civilization in the Congo. Nabil smiled as he read the words *civilization* and *Congo*—the same story of colonization repeating itself endlessly!

At first, he felt vindictive glee toward the Belgians. He also felt enlightened somehow as he saw the guile of history at work before his very eyes. The story of a Belgian soldier in the Congo had been transformed into another Congo in Belgium. Who was the winner? Once again, it was the guile of history. He laughed.

He kept walking until he hit Chaussée de Mons, a wide street crossed by the tramway. It held old houses, African bars, Turkish snack shops, and restaurants with signs written in Arabic that served hummus, falafel, and kebab.

Had he traveled all this way just to eat kebab? He laughed out loud at the thought. *Once again, the Arab déjà vu*, he thought. *It's the same thing—the same voices, the buildings all looking the same, and the restaurants offering the same dishes*. Nabil considered another idea from al-Farabi's understanding of Arabic music, which was based on repetition. The art of arabesque isn't a purely decorative art with infinite variations and inflexions. Rather, it reflects the Arabs' spiritual vision of the circularity of time and how it governs the universe. *What a philosophy!* He laughed, stopped, smiled, and then said aloud, "Who cares?!"

♪

As he walked on, the street became more and more crowded. He got to the butcher shop. On its huge door, with its dark red smears, he read the phrase, "Slaughtered according to Islamic tradition."

He wanted to go back to his apartment for fear of getting lost in the crowd. On his return, he saw a diner with the sign that read, "Chez Mohammad al-Maghribi." He entered and looked at the various dishes displayed behind the glass. He ordered a sandwich and some fries to go.

A television aired the news from al-Jazeera. The customers were Africans, Arabs, Turks, and Iranians. The waiter spoke Turkish. He prepared Nabil's sandwich quickly, put it in a plastic bag, and handed it to him. As he left, Nabil ran into a man in his fifties. With his beard dyed black, shaved moustache, and Afghani-style clothes, he exemplified the fashion of the new rebels, adopted by Salafis from the Afghan war against the Soviet army. Without turning, Nabil sensed that the Salafi was following him. As soon as he got to his place, the man grabbed him by the hand. Nabil looked back, terrified. The Salafi asked him, "Aren't you a Muslim?"

Shaking, Nabil replied, "Yes, I'm a Muslim."

"Then how can you eat, man? How can you eat?" He was angry, and Nabil was really confused.

"Is it forbidden for Muslims to eat?"

"Of course, it's forbidden. What will the infidels say about us?"

"How is it forbidden?"

"It's the month of Ramadan, man! Don't you know Ramadan?"

"Yes, I do. But we're in Belgium."

"If you come to Belgium, do you relinquish your Islam?"

"No, of course not. But forgive me, sir! I forgot it was Ramadan."

"Sure, I'll forgive you. But I'm not sure God will forgive you."

"I hope He will."

He wanted to run, but the man grabbed him by the hand again. "Where are you going?"

"Back to where I live."

"No, wait a minute. Listen, you made a mistake during Ramadan, and you have to pay a fine to be pardoned."

"I have to pay something as an atonement?"

"Yes, an atonement!"

Nabil's jaw dropped as the man went on, "You know there are many Muslims here. The mosque is too small for us now. We need to build another one, so we're asking for donations from Muslim residents. And since you're a Muslim who didn't observe Ramadan, as atonement for your wrongdoing, you'll have to pay a certain amount of money to contribute to the new mosque. Then God will forgive you. I guarantee it."

"I'll think about it. I have to see how much money I have. Then I'll let you know."

"Where do you live, exactly?"

"In this building!"

"Ah, you live next to one of our brothers. He's a very pious man. Listen, we'll stop by tomorrow to see how much you'll contribute."

Nabil left immediately and went up to his apartment. He

was agitated and perplexed. At first, he almost lost his cool. He put the bag on the table and went to the fridge. He opened it. There was nothing in it. He took a seat on the sofa and started eating his sandwich. He was a little bit thirsty. He thought back to his last beer in Baghdad and decided to go buy a few beers. He looked through the window and saw the Salafi leaving. Looking left and right, he noticed a pair of shoes dangling on a rope from the apartment above his. Unsettled, he wondered if someone was watching him.

He returned to his sandwich, emptied the fries onto a plate, and looked in the kitchen for some ketchup. He was determined not to pay a single penny to extremists, whether in Baghdad or here. But what a coincidence! What rotten luck! He had left his country because of them, and here he found them in his face again. How could this be?

XIII

An hour later Nabil left the apartment and walked to the end of Jaurs Street. He tried to avoid looking at the Salafi, who was standing on the corner. He came to a large boulevard called Avenue Vienne that was lined with grocery shops. He entered the store that was closest to the avenue. The store-owner, a Pakistani man, was helping people silently without moving a single muscle in his face. He bought four cans of beer, looking both ways to check if anyone could see him. Then he walked back via Bournet Street to Rue Sergent De Bruyne. He was only a few steps away from his place when a person hiding in a corner surprised him. "Are you a Muslim?"

Nabil didn't know what to say. He was at a loss. Judging from his light complexion, the person was a European with long blond hair pulled back and green eyes, but he wore old-fashioned clothes.

"Yes, I am. Why?"

"Do you sell pot?"

Nabil was even more confused. "No, I never do drugs."

"Don't worry, man, I wanna buy! I remember coming here once, and I bought from someone who lived in this building. He used to hang a big shoe with a rope from his window to signal that he had a big quantity for sale."

"Ah! Listen, the person who lives above me hung a shoe out an hour ago. I didn't know why."

"The shoe isn't there now; he must have run out. You know, these days Muslims don't drink because of Ramadan, so they look for pot instead."

Nabil was surprised. He didn't have anything to add. He looked at the desperate face of the blond guy and wished him luck.

He headed toward the building, opened the door, and climbed the dirty staircase, taking two stairs at a time.

XIV

Life wasn't that easy in Schaerbeek, the Turkish immigrant neighborhood, but it wasn't difficult either!

As he shaved off his moustache for the first time in his life, Nabil said to himself, "Jacques Brel was born in this neighborhood. Don't forget that! And the local market is just below the window. From early morning you can hear a vendor with an obvious Turkish accent crying, 'Grilled chicken, grilled chicken!' while the scent of clementine and avocado waft up to your room. Of course, none of this matters because the Utopian City has never materialized on earth from Plato's time to this day."

He wiped the hair off the blade with his hand and shook it under the running faucet. He stared at his face without a moustache. It was a little bit strange, but he could get used to it. As he put on his pants and shirt, he wondered: *What was lacking in the Utopian City al-Farabi imagined more than ten centuries ago? Harmony.*

This was Nabil's vision of society. He had picked it up from al-Farabi's theory on music. One sound alone can't produce music. Music is the sum of the difference between various sounds, and this difference requires perfect harmony. Otherwise, dissonance cancels out the basic principle behind its creation.

The road that led to the music shops in Saint Joyce was busy that day. A dignified old man explained to Nabil the features of the cello he showed him. Nabil didn't have enough money to buy it. He was saving up, one penny at a time. Never mind. He would return for it later. His life was on a slow path here in Europe, but he was making progress. At least he had obtained asylum in Belgium. He was now able to rent a small apartment in Schaerbeek, not far from Hacket Street in the Turkish immigrant neighborhood. He didn't choose to live there, but it was less expensive than the neighborhoods where locals lived. He also had a Belgian girlfriend, and that was important. Her name was Fanny.

♪

Nabil had met Fanny at a party at the Parvis de Saint-Gilles in the Maison du Peuple bar. Lenin used to read Russian and French newspapers there before the revolution. Now it was a bourgeois bar. Nabil wasn't much bothered by this, since that's how progress goes. At the end of the day, wealth is the goal of every revolution. An old man who had worked at another bar for many years before being laid off had invited him to the party.

The day of the party at Maison du Peuple was the man's last day of work. He felt like an old ballet dancer performing on her last night, knowing that the next day she would retire and fall into oblivion. Nevertheless, the man looked happy. Nabil greeted him warmly. Fanny stood next to him. Nabil greeted her as well. A few minutes later, he offered to get her a mojito. She accepted. He brought the drink and stood in front of her without saying a word. She was talking to another person when she took notice. She quickly left that person before finishing the conversation and moved toward Nabil, who handed her the drink.

"Cheers!" she said.

It was love at first sight for Nabil. Like any man from the East, he didn't think rationally in the presence of a half naked body. As for her, she came from a culture of Cartesian logic, although she had never read a single line from Descartes. She considered the matter pragmatically and saw in him a handsome young man and a talented musician who wanted to integrate into her society by any means. A utopian dreamer, like a musician in the clouds, he was obsessed with two things: utopia and the orchestra.

Nabil explained his vision to her, saying, "What I'm looking for in Europe is a fundamental, inner harmony. It's the idea of order that derives its precise meaning from classical music, which is what leads to the Utopian City."

"I don't get it," Fanny said with a smile.

"I'll give you an example," he said as he downed half a mojito. "Society is like an orchestra. The strings are white Europeans. They're the backbone of the orchestra, with the violin, the viola, the cello, and the bass. Then there are the Latins. They represent the woodwinds, such as the oboe, the flute, the clarinet, and the bassoon. Then come the Orientals—the Arabs, Turks, Persians, and Kurds. They represent the brass instruments: the trumpet, the horn, the trombone, and the tuba. The Africans are like drums and the Asians are like cymbals."

"Why not? Isn't this the idea put forth by the social sciences?"

Fanny put her glass on the table and started dancing with him. She liked his equation. It placed the Europeans at the top, and that sounded good to her. In this atmosphere of lights, mojitos, Marlboro cigarettes, flirtatious chatter, and the clicks of digital cameras, the feeling of love suddenly blossomed. It was a hot, suffocating summer evening. Fanny danced with him. She was wearing a blue skirt. Her soft skin beamed with light, her neck looked flute-like and her glances like those of a child. They sat facing each other, like two birds in two cages. He felt love for her at first sight. He didn't need to prove it. It was so clear, like a raindrop on the other side of the glass window that only gets bigger, following its course and never disappearing. He felt an important change in his feelings and body. He told her that he didn't like Arab women, whose existence revolved around expensive clothes, hair care and hairdos, makeup, painting their toenails, and reading women's magazines such as *Sayyidati* and *Hawwa*. They looked for the handsome sons of the bourgeois, who courted women in shopping malls. He told her that he loved her because he found her beautiful, sensitive, and fragile, like an intriguing Japanese painting. Arab women were dark-skinned and bulky, their thighs and breasts full of cellulite because they ate too much hummus. He guffawed.

♪

Nabil felt that his life with Fanny would be wonderful. He desired her a great deal, but it was also pragmatic. In exile there are many adjustments, and the meanings of things change, for example:

Work becomes wealth.

Love becomes sex.

Identity is reduced to a religion or a sect.

The homeland becomes something we defend without living in it, as well as a place we loathe without leaving it.

Nabil wanted to change this view of things, this way of life, without losing his desires, his fantasies, and his other concerns. He would be a dedicated lover to Fanny, and he would help her. He wanted to think positively. As an Easterner, he would get along well with her, and he would appreciate cultural differences as much as she did. Appreciation wasn't only about sex. It implied a deeper understanding. This was very simple. They would chat together and exchange stories about their lives. He would ask her about her day and her thoughts. He would tell her about music, al-Farabi, Utopia, the West, and migration. The thought made him shiver with delight. Clearly, he loved her. When he asked her to spend the night with him, she didn't make excuses like, "No, I can't, not the first night!"

She quickly picked up her bag, placed her hand in his, and accompanied him home.

XV

In his small apartment on Acht Street in Schaerbeek, Nabil and Fanny were united. His apartment was like a nest: cozy and comfy. Nabil sat on the sofa and browsed through his disc collection looking for suitable music to play on the record player. He waited for her while she was in the bathroom. He had prepared towels and soap for her. After locking the door, he removed his shirt and flung himself on the bed. She came out of the bathroom topless. She put the towel aside, lay next to him, and started cuddling with him. They were close to the window.

"Should we move away from the window?" he asked her.

"Don't worry about the window. Just think about me."

He kissed her and put his hand on her breast; she melted between his hands. She was warm and fragile, as though she were about to vanish under his touches. A few minutes later they undressed. He sat on the edge of the bed to remove his belt and his pants. She lifted her body, reached down and removed her pants and underwear all at once. He looked at her. She was wearing only her hose. She began to remove them, but he stopped her and stared at her body. "You're sexier with them on."

She smiled and hugged him. He ran his hand down her belly. Then she got the upper hand and grabbed him by the neck, and he returned the move. They were united. They spent hours in bed. Nabil stood naked before Fanny as he gulped down a full bottle of water because he had sweated so much. He hadn't considered the natural and cultural consequences of what happened. It was natural for Fanny to let out cries of pleasure during sex. She couldn't help it. She screamed and screamed without restraint. Nothing could stop her. That was her nature. Everyone in the building heard her. Some of them laughed out loud when they heard her voice and waited to hear its variations.

After each bit of silence, as they changed position, the screams got louder. Some neighbors were excited and enjoyed it, but others were angry. Nabil had never considered this part of Fanny's culture. He went back to the bed, rested his head on her chest, and started caressing her body. Her eyes sparkled as she relaxed on her back, her legs open and her flesh vibrant. For a few minutes, neither said anything. She lit two cigarettes and placed one between his lips and one between her own, and they fell back onto the bed as the smoke and the smell of their bodies mingled with the classical music rising from the player. Nabil stared happily at the ceiling until he fell asleep.

♪

In the morning, Nabil watched Fanny walking around naked. There was a surprising atmosphere of peacefulness around them, and he was impressed by the way she felt so comfortable in her own body. Fanny walked around completely naked, no bra or underwear. She smoked, read, and ate naked, now raising her leg and now lowering it. Never had Nabil seen this peaceful nakedness, not even in his most erotic dreams. It came from the essence and the spirit of nature. The afternoon hours passed, and Nabil lay in bed without saying anything. He was just a spectator looking at Fanny and her nakedness as she moved around in the narrow space of the room. He felt that the scenes he was witnessing shrank the old feelings he had brought with him, starving them, drawing the lifeblood out of them, then supplying them with endless stimulation and bringing them to a higher level of sensuality. However, this sensuality didn't cancel out passion and curiosity. Sex here was the opposite of what it was in the East. Instead of flourishing in the darkness, it thrived in the clear light of day, combined with noise, movement, scents, music, and perhaps alcohol and opium.

Who said the beauty of the body becomes decadent in nakedness? This is a stupid idea! Nudity is the materialization of realism. It's more like classical music insofar as it is real, while at the same time it reveals its abstract essence. It was a remnant of Renaissance aesthetics, which saw in nude art one of the ideals of humanity, something we should aspire to. The essence of classical thought lies in the belief that life is in harmony with nature.

♪

The next day Nabil came home late with Fanny, both of them half drunk and half high. Fanny paid the taxi driver while Nabil preceded her to the apartment door where, to his surprise, he found his Turkish neighbor waiting for him. The edges of his dark moustache were twisted upward, and his muscles were quite visible. He was a blacksmith with a powerful grip, which Nabil loathed because it was the opposite of the fine, delicate hand of the cellist.

The Turk said clearly to Nabil, "Sir, I won't hold you to account for what you do in your apartment, but the sounds your girlfriend makes have a huge impact on my family."

"I don't understand," said Nabil.

"When you have sex with your girlfriend, she lets out loud screams that the whole building hears. Forgive me, but I have modest teenage daughters, and we can't accept this situation."

Nabil replied shortly, "That's not my problem. It's not me who screams. It's her."

Fanny was approaching. When the Turk saw that she was a blond Belgian girl, he retreated and said to Nabil, "It's better if you talk to her."

Fanny asked, "What's going on? What does this guy want from you?"

Nabil explained the problem to her.

"This man is asking you not to scream when you have sex because he has teenage daughters, and he doesn't want them to know about this sort of thing."

Fanny was furious. "What, what?!" she yelled in the hallway loud enough for everyone to hear.

"I'm in my own country, and I can scream however I please. Whoever doesn't like it can take his daughters back to his country, where they'll hear nothing but the azan, but here I do as I please."

When they got to the apartment, Fanny decided to open all the windows so that anyone who hadn't heard her before would hear her now, and anyone who had heard her faintly would hear her loud and clear this time. She undressed under the light of the lamp and performed a striptease, throwing off her clothes piece by piece. Then she threw herself onto the bed with complete abandon, stretching her hand toward him.

"Take off your clothes and come over here," she said with a smile. "I'll let his daughters hear sounds they'll never forget."

A few moments later all the residents heard Fanny screaming in bed. Her screams battered the walls, not to mention the eardrums.

XVI

The next day, Fanny sat on the edge of the bed looking for a small piece of paper in her purse to show Nabil.

"Do you know Tina?"

"I don't remember . . . Who is she?"

"Oh, did you forget? Tina—we met her in the Lecoq bar, and you talked with her about music."

"Oh, yeah, I remember her. She has big boobs, she's sexy, with short skirts that show her butt."

"Oh, Nabil! Is that all you remember about women?"

"No, but . . . I remember her. What about her?"

"Listen, she's producing a program of chamber music in a nineteenth-century house south of Brussels. She told me that you're welcome to join the orchestra if you have a cello."

But even after a full year of collecting social assistance, Nabil hadn't been able to buy a cello. When Fanny offered to give him the money for a cello, he was ecstatic. He jumped up and down and embraced her until she cried to see him so happy. He had been dreaming of buying a cello ever since his instrument had been broken in Iraq.

♪

He took the money from her and went straight to the music store in Saint Josse. The shopkeeper was overjoyed to see him. For a long time, this young refugee had stood like a lover before this instrument. For months, he had looked at it and sighed. The old salesperson himself went to the display window to retrieve the instrument, placing it in a black case, while Nabil almost danced out of joy. Delighted, Nabil chattered meaninglessly. The owner was so moved by this scene, having observed how Nabil would stand in front of the instrument, unable to pay for it, that he gave him a special discount, which left Nabil with several euros in his pocket.

Nabil left the shop and headed home. On his way, he stopped by a large clothing store to look for a black suit for the chamber music concert. Then he went back home to put his cello in his apartment before joining Fanny at her workplace on Chaussée de Waterloo. They hoped to go to the movies at the Galleries de La Reine that evening.

But when he approached the apartment building, he felt something amiss. He saw his Turkish blacksmith neighbor with two other people standing at the building's front gate. As soon as Nabil arrived, they confronted him. The Turk asked him angrily, his twisted moustache trembling, "What are you carrying?"

"This is a cello."

"Ah, a cello! You want to play us a soundtrack to go with the porn movie you produce with your girlfriend."

One punch, and Nabil's glasses flew into the air and fell on the sidewalk.

A blacksmith's fist! Nabil thought. The blow he received to his eye made him lose his sight completely. The two other guys grabbed the cello, broke it, and threw it in pieces to the ground. Nabil managed to escape the blacksmith's grip, although a swift kick sent him tumbling two steps down the staircase. Then he got up, raced to the apartment, opened the door and disappeared inside.

♪

He went directly to the fridge, took some ice, and placed it on his eye. Then he went out on the balcony to see what had happened to his cello, and saw it broken on the ground. The Turk and his two friends had disappeared. Nobody was there except the guard, who collected the broken pieces of the cello in a plastic bag to throw in the building's trash can.

Part Two
Where is the Utopian City?

"I am from there. I am from here.
I am not there, and I am not here.
I have two names, which meet and part,
and I have two languages.
I forget which of them I dream in."
—Mahmoud Darwish

I

When he thought about the Utopian City and how it ought to be, Nabil also thought about the people around him. Who among them deserved to be in the Utopian City, and who didn't? He had to remove a great number of people from his list, and the first of these was the Turkish man who had hit him and broken his instrument.

Every day he selected people of various groups to include: athletes, musicians, artists, artisans, and philosophers, as well as some beautiful women.

Ah! As though they were the youth of Sparta!

This is how he wanted to establish his Utopian City.

Of course, these imaginary exercises were an attempt to understand people and get acquainted with the language. In addition to imagining people's lives, he did some research in the few books that he was able to get his hands on. He also read the obscure notes Fanny had kept since she was a teenager, a sort of journal of her life. Even though Nabil didn't like her ideas for the most part, she was more aware than he was of local politics in Europe. After the Turk had hit him and broken his instrument, Fanny had become more attentive to him than before. To alleviate his pain, she invited him to spend most of their shared time in her apartment.

He loved Fanny's beautiful apartment. It was located in one of the wealthy neighborhoods where native Belgians lived, unlike his poor apartment in the Turkish immigrant neighborhood. She displayed a photo of Nabil with his cello, taken back in Baghdad when he played in the National Symphony Orchestra, in the center of one wall, between a solid dark armoire and an elegant wooden desk from Ikea. He often sat in that corner to read books, as well as newspapers and old magazines that Fanny had bought from a secondhand market.

To achieve symmetry with the furniture along the facing wall, Fanny had placed two chairs and a rectangular table, which held various items—scissors, a small mirror, tweezers, and writing utensils. In the middle of the room there was a leather-upholstered wooden seat facing the television. Nabil spent long hours there thinking. If he leaned his head to the right, he could see through the window overlooking the park, allowing his vision to embrace the bright horizon and fresh greenery. From the same window, the sun's hot beams entered the apartment in the morning, staining the floor a strange purple color and flooding the room with a pale, shimmering light.

♪

As the days went by, Nabil started feeling that Fanny had become more open with him than before. Her physical beauty had begun to approach perfection. Indeed, she had turned into a marvel. Every time he looked at her, he felt that she had taken on a new form and a new grace. He became accustomed to seeing her in the morning when they woke, in the afternoon when she came home from work, and in the evening after she returned tired from her Arabic class. She was studying Arabic in order to learn more about Nabil and his culture. At night, when he made love to her under the light of a beautiful lamp or a sweetly scented candle, which he usually bought from the Hema department store at the end of their street, she would scream as loudly as she liked.

Most of the time Nabil felt happy, as if catapulted high into the sky. But at other times he was distraught and pained because the Utopian City that was based on the values of justice, virtues, and music did not exist even in Europe. His only solace in Europe was Fanny. Seeing her refreshed him. Her eyes inspired him with joy. They sparkled with happiness at every encounter, whether at the coffee shop with her friends or when they were in bed. Fanny was his hands and feet. She solved all his administrative problems with the city. She talked with the bank, the police, and the tax administration, and she did all the difficult administrative errands that he didn't understand. She had become like an electric lamp to a Bedouin living in the darkness of the desert. This situation reminded him of some verses of poetry he had written before and put to music. They were about the gaze of a woman that casts intense, translucent rings of light onto a man who turns to stone before her.

"Isn't that Medusa?" Fanny asked him.

"Uhh, no," he said. But he wasn't sure. Then he continued reading some of the verses.

II

As Nabil started frequenting Fanny's place, he came to prefer it over his own. There was no Turk living downstairs with virgin daughters who couldn't be allowed to hear Fanny's voice as she cried out in the pleasure of love. She could scream as she pleased in her apartment. She had total freedom to scream or sing in her bed, out of pleasure or anything else, without him having to apologize to anyone or have an argument with anyone. In addition, and this was more important, Fanny's place was located close to Flagey Square and its famous Café Belga, which became his favorite hangout.

♪

Nabil started to hang out in Flagey Square. There he met all Fanny's friends and her former college classmates, who were regulars of Café Belga. But for some reason he switched to Pitch Pin, another café on the same square. It was a nice, spacious café that overlooked two street corners, with waitresses from Eastern Europe, and it was less crowded than all the other cafés on the square.

Nabil spent most of his time there drinking beer and reading about music or the Utopian City. Sometimes he would sit outside the bar, observing the dynamics in the square, which usually became crowded in the afternoon. He liked looking through the café windows at the tramways, buses, and people throughout the different times of day and seasons of the year.

He started getting acquainted with Brussels the way he would with a book he was reading. He knew the faces of the waiters, the coffee shop owners, the students, the actors, the prostitutes, the customers, and even the guards who worked across the square at the radio station. There he got acquainted with female newscasters, secretaries, and even bathroom attendants.

Every day he went either with Fanny or by himself to the bars and coffee shops of Brussels so that this beautiful city that had welcomed him might always be present in his heart and mind. When he went to bed in the evening, the scenes from each day remained engraved in his mind, as if they were inscriptions in a book he would read to Fanny.

"Did you see the girl who came to the café today? They say she's a prostitute."

"Did you see that handsome guy? He works with the European delegation. His girlfriend is Dutch. I saw her smoking pot once."

"Did you know that the waitress is a student at the Free University of Brussels? She's dating a rich American twenty years her senior!"

♪

Little by little Nabil got used to the cold weather, the damp streets, and the rainy evenings. Even late at night he would go to Flagey Square, Saint-Gilles, or Pl. Saint-Géry, where there were many bars, coffee shops, bookstores, and music stores. Sometimes he went out at night just to run errands, returning to his place or to Fanny's laden with books and records, a bottle of wine, or a red or white rose. This latter he would buy from an Indian or Bengali vendor that sold flowers in bars. When he went back home, everyone who saw him must have thought he had received an unexpected transfer of funds from his family or from some relative who lived in America. In fact, Nabil got his money from Fanny to buy useful things like books and cassettes. Then he would keep the change in his pocket for drinks, especially beer, which he had enjoyed drinking in the afternoon since his arrival in Belgium.

♪

Sometimes Nabil went barhopping, and usually ended up at Café le Coq near the stock market with a few euros still in his pocket. He would sit by groups of female foreign students or some rural girls looking for men like him to buy them a drink or two. He would regale them with the same stories, like the story of the Turk who hit him because of his girlfriend's noisy expressions of pleasure. He would explain to them his unique theories about Europe, Muslims, and immigrants. And when they found out that he had spent the last euro in his pocket, they would leave him there. He would return to Fanny, who would usually be awaiting him in Flagey, her eyes fixed on the door.

♪

This beautiful girl often worried about him when he disappeared. She would sit waiting for him in a remote corner of the bar. Everyone knew she was a beautiful girl, attractive and sensitive, from the village of Wallonia. She would spend hours waiting for her refugee boyfriend, who would disappear frequently without telling her where he had gone. She would order a drink without touching it, and stare at young men walking by her table, or she would look through the window for him. Many guys wondered who she was waiting for. Many would give her a nod or a smile, hoping she would leave her table and join them, but she never wavered.

However, after having a good time, Nabil would come back home half intoxicated. And it only made matters worse when he tried to console her. He was a nice guy and wanted her to feel good. But this just angered her.

"You don't need to feel that you neglect me. Don't feel guilty!"

"Are you sure?"

"Yes, you don't have to worry."

"I just wanted you to feel free," he said to her in a soft voice, but Fanny bristled.

"Nabil, I don't need you to make me feel free. I'm free already."

"Yes, you are free. I just wanted you to be free."

"Oh my god, you make me so mad when you speak like this. You're not making any sense. Don't you have something else to talk about?"

"You're unhappy with me."

"Nabil, would you be quiet? You're drunk."

"Do you think I drank too much?"

He put his arm around her, but she was totally lost. She had told him not to feel guilty because of her, but she looked annoyed. Her face darkened when he left her alone in a café while he went to flirt with other women.

III

On bitter cold days when the weather turned cloudy and gray, Nabil found refuge in cozy cafés. He was planning to spend an hour or two at Café Belga before having dinner with Fanny. The place was filled with the glow of female students, who gathered near the entrance almost every day. When it rained, they met inside the café. Not only was it a cozy, warm place, but it was flooded with the smell of their perfume. They fluttered under the dimmed light like beautiful butterflies. Those without a male companion would stroll out to the street to smoke or to chat with passersby, and then return to their seats.

♪

One day Nabil got totally drunk. Fanny had gone out with a girlfriend, and her wallet remained with him. She had told him, "Nabil, I'm leaving my wallet here in my bag."

He said confidently, "OK, sure, leave it there."

He was talking to two female students in a darkened corner, and the wine went to his head. Next to him sat a group of five people: three guys and two female clarinet players. They chatted on and on.

Nabil wowed them all with his words. He was a brilliant conversationalist, and as he talked, he felt happier and in need of more wine. He reached for Fanny's wallet in her bag. He was penniless, but he ordered drinks for everyone.

"Eight more glasses of beer and wine!"

"Are you serious?" one girl asked him.

Most of the students who were there were from poor and rural backgrounds. They lived frugally in Brussels and were delighted to see him so generous. He ordered a dark beer for himself, the kind they make at monasteries, with a higher percentage of alcohol. He downed the beer quickly, then ordered two big drafts of Duvel beer and downed them just as fast. The drinks he offered to the students made them all listen to him and made all the girls look and smile at him politely, even though nobody understood his complex French phrases and the elitist words he pronounced with an Iraqi accent that none of them had ever heard before.

This encouraged him to order one round after another. They drank and laughed as he talked about immigrants in a loud voice. All his jokes were about immigrants, in particular the story about the Turk, his virgin daughters, and the cello that had been broken by extremist neighbors both in Baghdad and in Belgium.

When Fanny returned, she was shocked to see Nabil so drunk that he was crawling from table to table, inviting everyone who listened to him to have a beer, a glass of wine, or even a cocktail. She found her wallet empty except for a few pennies.

Horrified, she watched him struggling unsuccessfully to get to his feet, with no one trying to help. Fanny was terrified by the indifference of the bar customers. She heard some people whispering, "Leave him alone. He's just a refugee. He stole his girlfriend's wallet and squandered everything in it."

IV

The next day Nabil woke up early; he wanted to go to the kitchen to pour himself a glass of water. He was thirsty, his mouth was dry, and he had a terrible headache. Fanny was asleep, sprawled half naked on the bed. The clock on the nightstand near her head continued its tick-tock, and some morning light sifted into the room through the curtain. He looked down at his feet as he held on to the edge of the bed and tried to find his sandals without making any noise. But it was in vain. He knew he was clumsy. Fanny likened him to a bull in a China shop. He would always break something when he walked around, as he had no sense of distances and proportions. He'd bump into the table, or the bed, or unintentionally slam the door.

"You have no sense of your body's proportions," she once said.

He admitted as much. "Usually, the image I have of my body is smaller than reality."

"How can that be?"

"I don't know, but when I walk, I bump into stuff."

Nabil thought about what had happened the night before. He had better explain it to Fanny when she woke up. He would have to choose his words carefully and express his thoughts properly. But how to do that? Every time he tried to come up with an idea, the hangover prevented him from finishing it. He didn't feel sober enough to think about what

had happened. His head throbbed, especially when he tried
to move his head or open his eyes.

What happened last night in the bar? he asked himself.

He thought about the accusing look in her eyes the previous day. He remembered how she had looked at him as she
helped him get into the cab and climb the stairs when they
came back home. She must have been irritated. He knew her
all too well now, having lived with her. She could be frank,
but most of the time he couldn't tell what she was thinking.
She always confused him with the contradictions between
her facial expressions and the reality of her feelings. She
smiled when she was mad, and frowned when she was happy.

When they came back home, she didn't say a word. She
washed his face for him and offered him some water to alleviate the hangover. This was helpful and he quickly recov-
ered his spirits. As soon as they lay down naked on the bed,
he got closer to her. They made love without her saying a
word to him. When they were done, she turned the lights on
and grabbed an old Belgian comic book by Georges Remi,
better known as Hergé. She placed the book on her naked
breasts and started reading. Before he fell asleep, Nabil gave
Fanny a little smile. She smiled back, but it was tepid, and he
knew it wasn't from her heart. He turned to give her a good
night kiss, but his nose bumped hers. She wiped her nose
without kissing him back and went back to her reading. He
remained silent for a while and then fell asleep.

♪

The apartment was very quiet. The outside world hadn't woken yet. There were no sounds of the tramway or cars outside. It was still too early for Fanny to go to work. He knew she usually slept very lightly and that if she woke up, she could not go back to sleep, or it could take her a long time to fall asleep again.

Nabil understood that Fanny had a job and needed to have enough sleep time. She was very strict about her wellness time; it was sacred. She could be flexible with many things, but not with her relaxation time. He knew that even though they lived together, she had her own private life, her own world, and that she didn't allow anyone to interfere with that. Her wellness time, her reading time, her entertainment, and her family time, as well as her travel time with him or with her friends were all part of her own private domain. When she met him, she asked him to respect these boundaries. Since they had started living together, he had come to realize that her sleep time was very important to her, and he tried his best not to disturb her. If she woke up before she was supposed to, she became moody and upset with him.

He once commented to a friend, "It's not easy to live with a roommate here. All couples realize that. Sharing life together is a difficult thing. Even if you're open-minded, you'll always have problems. You need to make concessions and the other person also needs to do the same. It's not that easy."

That day, Nabil looked in the mirror in the dim light of the lamp. He noticed the color of his eyes, his prominent cheek bones, and his forehead, where he could see the sleepless

nights and how many cigarettes he had smoked from the
color of his lips. He was looking older as the years passed.

♪

Fanny knew all too well that Nabil was always lost in his
thoughts, always adrift. He didn't focus on people or what
they did. Even when it came to their life together, he was present and not present at the same time. He came from a large
family where his parents and his siblings all lived together in
the same house. He was used to rooming with six other people, not just one. In the East, nobody really cared about the
idea of individuality. But Fanny's arrangements with Nabil
were different: despite the love and the passion, she was very
strict when it came to her personal, private life. When he
thought about the meaning of individuality, Nabil realized
that in the East, no matter how liberated and enlightened a
family was, and even if they were graduates of Arab or in-
ternational universities, there was no room for individuality
for either men or women. Private space was easily infringed
upon.

Things were easier for him. He didn't care when he slept
or woke up. He could sit at the table or stretch out on the sofa
in the living room. Fanny would find him standing on the
balcony, sipping tea or coffee, or drinking a beer and smoking. When she came in the living room, he would be facing
her, reading, writing his musical compositions, or engrossed
in listening to a phonograph record.

Once Fanny shared with a friend of hers that her life with
Nabil was quite good. Often when she returned from work,

she would find that he had prepared a Middle East vegetarian dish that she liked, such as hummus, falafel, and baba ghanoush. Fanny was vegetarian. As for Nabil, he was vegetarian only when he ate with her. But if he happened to be invited to a meal where there was meat, he would have no problem. He was vegetarian only on occasion. However, he was a true lover, a true musician, and an authentic artist, and this is what she loved about him. He was sincere in his emotions, and because of this she forgave many of his shortcomings.

V

Nabil admitted to Fanny that sometimes he was still awkward with others. Unlike what people thought, this wasn't because he was a refugee or an immigrant. But every time he behaved oddly, people turned away from him with scorn and disgust, and stigmatized him as an immigrant or a refugee. He knew they made these sweeping judgements carelessly and routinely about all those who didn't look like them or who spoke with an accent. But Nabil wanted to be treated differently from other refugees. He wasn't like an immigrant, a refugee, or even someone in exile. The problem was that people used these words unthinkingly, without nuance, and sometimes in a hostile way. Consequently, he found these words offensive, cruel, and humiliating. They were a weapon in the hands of amateurish white people, who used them to attack him. Every day he wondered, why is it that they don't know other words? Do they use them impulsively, or intentionally? Usually, the words "immigrant" and "refugee" did not occur out of context, and most of the time they were targeted at him. People stuck them on his forehead like a label on a tin can, sometimes using them to explain his behavior and contradictions.

But Nabil saw things differently. For him, his eccentricity was part of who he was as an artist. He saw it as a mark of distinction and a departure from the average taste. Regardless of how deviant it might be from norms and conventions, it wasn't bad or ugly. It was musicality, a leap into the unknown, a kind of creativity. Wasn't creativity about the unusual and the uncommon? Wasn't it something different from what was generally recognized and accepted? Therefore, and despite many people's condemnation of what he had done the day before, he wasn't hurt or degraded by it. On the contrary, it elevated him above average people and made him special. He knew this world was full of foolish and ignorant people. No one people or nation has a monopoly on stupidity. Nabil always repeated this to those who didn't believe him. Yes, there were a lot of foolish people here too. They thought his behavior was caused by his cultural ignorance of Europe, because he was a new refugee, someone fresh off the boat. Therefore, they assumed he had no clue about the lives of white people, no idea about their virtues and their merits. This infuriated him. It revolted him and made him scream, "I'm not an immigrant! That word doesn't describe me at all. I'm on my own turf. Isn't this the land of classical music? Brahms, Handel, Beethoven, Debussy, Mahler—these are my brothers, and we all breastfed from the same mother: music, the daughter of this land, the daughter of the West!"

But how to explain this to the taxi driver, the municipal employee, or the neighbors, let alone the vegetable vendors, the police and all the white people he interacted with daily? Who among them even knew the names of these musicians? Who cared what Nabil loved or hated?

For Nabil, the artist didn't emigrate. Rather, he was a migrant in thought and imagination. After all, thought doesn't settle in one place, and imagination doesn't live in a single land or under one sky. Ideas travel, and imagination has no limits. Nabil's imagination was cosmic, and his music was both Western and universal. It was not just for a particular nation or group. True, it was the product of a particular culture and a specific geography, but it was universally adopted. Therefore, Nabil shouldn't be judged by the place where his body was born, but by the birthplace of his spirit and the place where his imagination grew. *Yes*, Nabil thought. *My spirit was born in the kingdom of classical music. Classical music is Western and so is my personal culture. But classical music is also universal, and anyone who understands it and trains in it can take pride in that. It isn't the sole province of one group of people. It belongs to humankind. It doesn't just consist of music and emotion, but vision as well. People can think and see the world through it. It's a method and a way of life and knowledge.*

So how could Nabil be described? Quite simply, he was a classical musician, a romantic, a modernist, and many other things, but not an immigrant or a refugee. There was no connection between his behavior and the fact that he was "an immigrant." As an artist, he felt he had license to do what others weren't allowed to. This may have been overconfidence on his part, and he knew this. However, this confidence made him comfortable when speaking. There was also his insight and the power his talent gave him, the talent for using an instrument that not many people could play the way he could.

VI

There had always been a corner of Nabil's brain that was open to the outside world, even when he was in Baghdad. He would start his day early in the morning listening to classical music. He loved the aesthetics of German composers such as Bach, Handel, Beethoven, Brahms, Strauss, Mendelssohn, Schumann, and Wagner, which accorded with the thought of Germany's great philosophers such as Hegel, Fichte, Kant, Schelling, Nietzsche, Schopenhauer, and Marx. Who else had expressed themselves as boldly as they had? He called these composers' productions Western music, and even Eastern European musicians like Tchaikovsky, Rachmaninoff, and Scriabin, he classified as Western, just as he placed himself in the West, even though he was not born there.

To Nabil, values were like a ladder that one had to climb. This ladder was not specific to a particular nation, but it happened to be concentrated in one place, or on a particular soil. Thanks to certain historical circumstances, this one soil had allowed these noble values and virtues to grow and thrive. Sources could come from different places, but the soil was stable, and right now it corresponded to the West. Where was this soil exactly? In the beginning, Nabil thought it was in the West, but when he landed in the Western country of "Belgium," he suffered a setback, and changed his mind. He found that the West didn't have the aesthetic harmony he had imagined it to have, with both a great philosophy and classical music, the two mirroring each other. This beautiful equation had been shaken because of the economy.

Nabil hated economics, capitalism, the accumulation of profit, and competition. The economy was what stood in the way of aesthetic harmony and prevented it from attaining perfection. The economy had created colonialism, the ugliest development in Western thought. The economy was a dissonant note in this great symphony that had come out of Europe. The economy was the cause of all the cacophony in Western history: colonialism, world wars, poverty, exploitation, and so on. And now it was the cause behind the collapse of Nabil's vision and his hope of seeing a beautiful world, free of the dissonance that destroyed harmony and prevented the emergence of the Utopian City.

Sitting with his face in his palms, Nabil lamented hopelessly, "The theory is beautiful and harmonious, but the world is full of contradictions." Where was the Utopian City that he had believed to be in the West? Well, geographically speaking, it could no longer be said to be in the West. But it still existed as a concept, an eternal idea, without limits or boundaries. It lived on in the hearts of those who believed in it. Standing up with a sigh of relief, he walked to the fridge, looking for a glass of cool water.

VII

At night, Nabil listened to his inner voice, the voice of his soul that had been shaped by music. When he composed music, he paced up and down his room as he used to do in Baghdad. He looked out at the garden through his room's window in his parents' house. He liked watching the birds gobbling down mulberries, the cat jumping over the fence, and the dogs peacefully wandering the streets. This world was infinite music, but humans were blinded by the quest for their livelihood. The fear of not having enough food and sex made people kill each other. It made them care more about missiles than about music. Now, as before in Baghdad when he used to spend the hot, dust-filled days and the fiery evenings writing a musical piece in his head, he saw the world around him only partially. He was half blind. He didn't care about the outside world as much as he cared about himself. He didn't work to make money. He could get that from his family, his girlfriend, or social services. The world needed to respect him as he aimed to rescue it. Art, not the economy or politics, would save the world from its lowliness. Not even religion could do that. The ideal world that art could create would save humanity. Art would unite humanity because it had a universal language with an abstract meaning that was shared by all humans. And unlike human languages that could be overused and worn out, the language of art could never be exhausted. Art was universal because it spoke to the authentic human nature shared by all. Art was the eternal perfection that would displace religion. This was how Nabil thought. Was he infatuated with himself? He was indeed.

Fanny was completely aware of this. Even though she seemed not to care much about the nature of his personality, she was consciously and discretely observing his behavior. She had read some of what he was writing about himself after discovering a suitcase full of papers. It contained remarks he had written down and musical notes he had composed. There were also some newspaper and magazine clippings, and announcements he had saved. All these things together revealed his personality. Fanny told her friend, "Nabil is a good man. He's innocent, sincere, and naïve, but he's arrogant and vain in his opinions. He has great respect for his talent, but a horrible hatred for his origin. How can he solve this problem? That's what makes me worry about him."

In fact, Fanny was right. Nabil hated Brabant market, a popular market that sold the same kind of clothes one could find in Arab markets. He told her this was a big mistake, since the clothes sold in this market were of the same bad quality many poor people wore in the Arab world. When immigrants arrived in Brussels, they would buy these garments and wear them in Europe and feel as if they were still living in their countries of origin. He said the government should ban such apparel, since it clashed with the country's national dress.

"This country has no national dress," she replied.

"Yes, it does! And there should be high-quality standards for the clothes the government imports. The government shouldn't let this shabbiness spread all over the place. The immigrants and refugees who come to this country look in this market for the same type of clothes they used to wear in their countries of origin. Then they look for housing in neighborhoods of their own, only for these neighborhoods to end up looking like ghettos."

"No one can force them to live in specific areas."

"Okay, let's say it is a ghetto by choice, where they wear the same clothes, eat the same food, and marry among themselves. Let's ban them from living here. People are short-sighted. They get absorbed in their environment. When I visit some places in Brussels, I don't see that they belong to this city. They could just as easily be in the Arab world, China, or Africa. This is very disappointing. The government should restrict the kind of clothing that comes into Europe. The people who frequent Brabant Market and the merchandise you find there make you feel as if you were in Morocco or in Turkey."

"What does the government have to do with that? People should be free to wear what they like."

"But I think this is a big mistake."

"What's wrong with it, Nabil?"

"Listen, I'll explain my theory about that."

He began pacing up and down his room as he used to do back in Iraq when he would think up a new idea or talk about a project.

Then he started explaining his theory, saying, "The way people dress reflects their self-perceptions. When these people dress like that, it makes them identify with a different people than the people who live here. When people come to Europe and dress and eat like they used to in their home countries, this means they'll remain connected with that other country and there won't be any change in their lives."

"And why would you want them to make any changes to their lives?"

"So that they can integrate into the new society and be one with us."

"They can be one with us in spirit and mind, not in the way they dress."

"That won't happen!"

"What? Why not?"

Nabil walked up and down as he explained his ideas to Fanny, his thin lips muttering as if he were creating a musical melody, and his grey eyes gazing into the void. He told her that the person who wore ragged clothes or even sports clothes would not handle himself and the things around him the same way as a person who wore elegant clothes, such as formal attire with an ironed shirt, a necktie, and a jacket. When he walked, the former wouldn't care if he got mud on his shoes, or if he walked into a puddle or next to the trash can, whereas the person who wore expensive, elegant clothes would calculate his every step.

"Oh, Nabil, that's rubbish."

"No, it's not. Imagine a conductor wearing blue jeans and a tank top."

"I wouldn't care. I might think it was sexy."

"Imagine a rock 'n' roll musician wearing a smoking jacket and a bowtie."

"That would be funny, but cute."

"You're saying that just to disagree with me."

"It's not that I disagree, but you sometimes give examples that have nothing to do with the topic."

♪

One day Nabil went out to pick up some things from his apartment in the immigrant neighborhood. He was annoyed by the noise of children playing soccer in the street as well as the car horns mixed up with the noise of human voices. He crossed the street where there were Arab, Turkish, Indian, and even Bulgarian cafés. A horde of workers headed to the pubs where the smell of French fries filled the air. A group of men with oily hair, tired faces, and pointed moustaches sat around dishes piled with appetizers lined up on white marble tables. There was yogurt with cucumber, liver grilled Turkish style, stewed green beans, brain, and arugula salad. He felt strangely dizzy and almost fainted. He couldn't stand these Middle Eastern dishes anymore. They reminded him of rancid cooking oil and strong beer that smelled like horse urine.

VIII

Fanny didn't quite agree with Nabil. She sometimes found his ideas farfetched. Things were different for him as he tried to find connections in his mind between incongruous things. He always managed to organize incompatible elements into one congenial sequence, like arranging different voices into a harmonious texture. But he always failed when he applied this theory to human beings. Yet, he supported dialogue, which he saw as a kind of concerto.

"What?" Fanny asked him. "How is that possible?"

Nabil was thinking of doing a lot of things, including composing a cello concerto in three movements entitled *Musician in the Clouds*, showcasing his relationship as a refugee with the new society in which he wanted to integrate.

"It's a musical dialogue between the cello and the orchestra that tries to say things through music, a musical pursuit in broad and wavy strokes where the cello tries to convince the orchestra of the validity of its ideas."

"This means you will be in conversation with others."

"Yes, I engage society through the cello. In the beginning, the cello or I will introduce new ideas different than the society or the orchestra's ideas. Usually this is a fast movement, *allegro*. Then I calm down a bit and I engage in a slow, emotional movement called *andante*. In the final movement, I come back very fast, *prestissimo*, where I use all my technical skills to convince the orchestra. In this last movement I play a cadenza."

"What is a cadenza?"

"It's a part of the concerto where I play a solo in which I show all my creative talent to convince society of the soundness of my ideas, just as the cello convinces the orchestra with its technical prowess."

Fanny smiled at Nabil. That was a happy and wonderful day. Here was something that Nabil could focus his attention on. She realized that he was a real artist: a bit eccentric, but sincere. Somewhat naïve, but kind. He was a mixture of clairvoyance and dark humor, a peaceful soul and sublime inspiration. He was a poet and an absurdist at the same time, full of ideas and always ready for new ones that he soon fell for. An absent-minded, eastern wanderer. He was like a reservoir of sweet, clear water that wasn't fit to drink.

IX

In the beginning of summer, Nabil and Fanny lay down under the giant trees in a park called Le Bois de la Cambre. Like two flowers with butterflies hovering around them, they quietly immersed themselves in the woods amid the foliage. With a nail he'd found on the ground, Nabil carved their names on a brown tree trunk. They discovered mysterious paths and enjoyed chasing the rabbits into their hideouts. They felt completely relaxed. Silence surrounded them in the beautiful weather. They breathed in and enjoyed the atmosphere of the forest. Suddenly a memory flashed through his mind: he was lying on the ground in a war zone in Iraq, his arms folded behind his neck and his legs stretched out.

He was very happy now. He took a Heineken beer out of their picnic bag and started sipping it. He felt exalted and full of energy. His thoughts flew far away, and his soul circled freely in space. He felt as if he were in a terrestrial paradise, full of love and desire for life, his musical goals, and other things he wanted to achieve. Life on this earth couldn't be reduced to a single thing. There were extraordinary, positive forces inside him: love, desire, the will to create peace, a longing for beauty. There were also destructive forces that turned him into a fool, but which, luckily, were neutralized by art. He knew nature wasn't always fair: it gave the upper hand to men over women, and to the rich over the poor. But culture could balance things out and correct the course, and art was the instrument of culture.

♪

Nabil had a keen desire to express his appreciation for Brussels. It gave him this inner peace that made him feel gratitude and an eternal attachment to beauty. It gave him loads of energy and made him appreciate and enjoy the sun, which he had hated in his country. A few days earlier, he had found himself writing a poem in French and had given it to Fanny to correct it. She had liked it a lot and edited the language a bit. The poem went like this:

Goodbye, my soldier friends who died in the Iraqi
*   American war.*
Goodbye to my writer friends who were slaughtered by
*   terrorists.*
Goodbye to the sad palm tree next to our house.
I have decided not to die near you.
Your death is tragic and miserable.
I have decided to die in my new country like an
old Flemish farmer whose grip is firm and his head hard;
like a dark-skinned Walloon laborer who for a long time
*   worked*
in the mines and in his retirement sat down under a tree to
drink his beer and eat his cheese.
I will die here in my new country without church bells or
*   holy books.*

It will suffice for a young Belgian woman to
throw a single flower on my tomb, and for a bird to grace it
with its warm droppings in the morning.
And if I don't get these two things,
let a handsome young man who drank a
lot of beer in the bar pee on the cemetery fence.
God will then forgive all my sins.
My life in the country of beer and
chocolate has taught me that only the mad and the foolish
believe in heroism.

X

Nabil told Fanny that Brussels was the only way he could achieve climax in music. He loved this town and identified with it even more than its natives did. He told her this often, saying he still could not understand what Edward Said meant when he said that exiled people were anxious and unsure about their identity in the new place. He explained that this was a luxury of intellectuals, just fancy words. Edward Said was more of a New Yorker than any person who'd been born there.

"But that wouldn't keep people from feeling anxious," Fanny commented.

Nabil made no comment, but he definitely wasn't convinced of her argument. At the very least, he wanted to ask her why he, Nabil, wasn't anxious. She might have replied that each human experience was different. Or perhaps she would have said, "You're anxious, but you won't admit it."

Nabil didn't want to argue with her. Every time they argued, he lost the debate. She knew very well that he had a strong sense of his own idiosyncrasies, and he recognized that there were contradictions between what he said and the truth of the matter. He always explained this by saying that people have more than one truth, and that imagination and introspection add freshness and flexibility to ideas, without which these contradictions end up dry, shrill, and even extremist. In the beginning, she was shocked by his contradictions. As soon as he heard someone talking about Iraq, he would start to brag about it. She knew that Iraq was the cradle of civilization, that all the progress of current civilizations was the result of the achievements of Mesopotamian civilization. She knew that Arab civilization was of an equal grandeur with European civilization. They both had monotheistic religions, while Arab civilization had built mighty empires and made great scientific contributions to humankind.

Was there something wrong? For Nabil, nothing was wrong here. These weren't passing ideas. They were part of his life. When he was in Iraq, he had been very ambitious. He had been a member of the most advanced music movement there. In his childhood, he had won the Art Association Award, an annual award dedicated to the best and most authentic historic music that represented the Mesopotamian past. This was part of an effort to build a national conservatory that could compete with schools in European countries. He had studied in a conservatory where most of the professors were Europeans. It was a prestigious school built in the 1930s by the King of Iraq, and was meant to display the intellectual vigor, heroic virtue, and wisdom of the Iraqi people. This was the tradition Nabil was so attached to. Later, he thought about composing a symphony inspired by the myth of Gilgamesh, but he hadn't been a fully realized artist at that point. He needed to deepen his musical study before embarking on his ambitious project.

"I've really worked hard to achieve a harmonious mind."

"But you haven't succeeded," Fanny said.

"Maybe I've been driven by an unknown longing, an unconscious desire that I've submitted to. This has led to fantastic results when it comes to music."

"Yes, it may work in terms of musical achievements, but not when it comes to life itself."

"I want to turn this energy into concrete expressions that sound as natural as possible."

"Be careful, though. They're not natural. You use many expressions that make people angry."

♪

In the following days, Nabil thought a lot about what Fanny had told him. He agreed with some of what she had said. It was true that he often used blunt and harsh words that could be upsetting, but he never meant to provoke or belittle people. They weren't an attack on others, and it was nothing personal. For him, ideas were something in the public domain, available, wide open, and free. They weren't targeted at any individual. But who was going to understand Nabil or forgive him his intellectual musings?

XI

Nabil was an artist. He wasn't bigoted, and Fanny was liable to be incredibly influenced by his ideas. After she edited his poem, she waited for him in the living room looking happy and relaxed. Her beautiful features deserved praise: she was slender and tall. Nabil was short. Her face was radiant, while his was pale. He didn't look rural and didn't have the characteristic looks of an Arab. It was difficult to pin him down. He was dark-skinned, an excellent reader, a stay-at-home guy, with pleasant qualities. He was generous, with a childlike soul. Small things could make him happy.

His sense of happiness might be strange, but as soon as he felt happy, Nabil would make everyone around him feel the same. This was also one of his greatest ideas about classical music, that it was a tool to make all of humanity feel happy and peaceful. It saved them from their earthly condition and put them into an exquisite, ethereal place. It lifted them off the ground by a degree. Throughout human history, a sense of contentment has multiplied achievements, and this is what he thought of as the mission of classical music. Its message was not to be connected to any articulated language, because language would tie it down to a particular nation, a particular culture, and a people who speak and understand that language. Instead, music was a self-sufficient language, without articulated words. Even in operatic singing, one could listen to undulations of the voice, its beauty and performance, without the need to understand the language and its meaning. It was true that mad tyrants had weaponized music and diverted it from its goals, such as when Hitler made soldiers and officers on the war front listen to Wagner's music, or when Stalin streamed Shostakovich's symphony *Leningrad* during the siege of Saint Petersburg of World War II. But this didn't alter the peaceful nature of classical music and its goal of spreading happiness in people's hearts.

♪

Nabil believed that artists have to invent themselves. This was no easy job. He would become a star. Is this what he wanted? Perhaps he would just retreat into himself and his personal myth because he was unable to communicate directly and painlessly even with the people closest to him. For sure, the aspiration for perfection was part of his soul's great yearning and his personal need to establish a new legacy. His family of origin didn't mean much to him anymore. He wanted to belong to a new family, here, in Europe. He wanted to create a family. These pursuits were not free of feelings of guilt and anxiety, but they also brought him pleasure and happiness. In his family, he was the son who had gone astray. Leaving the Arab world had alienated him. However, it had also brought an end to everything that burdened him: the constant threat, fear of punishment, fear of the authorities, the terror of religious clerics, the police, the society, almost everything.

♪

Fanny pointed out to him that he was full of contradictions. "On the one hand you want to separate from your culture, but as soon as you hear someone talk about Iraq, you start expressing your pride in its culture and its civilization."

She was right.

One day, Nabil decided to forget the Arabic language, change his name, and speak French only, without using a word of Arabic when he talked to people. He distanced himself from anything Arabic or Islamic. He broke away from his people's painful, sad news, their miserable lives, and their nonsense politics, as he used to call it. He became interested in European politics, especially Belgian politics. When Fanny called him Nabil, he wouldn't respond. He told her that from now on, his new name was Martin. But one day Martin got sick and was assailed by the Arabic language. This broke his nerves. Arabic words and poetic verses and phrases stormed his dreams. It was a linguistic nightmare par excellence. When he woke up, he was breathless, drenched in cold sweat as fever crept into his limbs.

"What's with you?" Fanny asked him in alarm as he woke up exhausted.

"I think I'm sick."

"You were speaking in Arabic."

He looked at her frightened. "The Arabic language is taking its revenge on me. I tried to forget it, but it seems that's impossible."

♪

He realized that it was impossible to win victory over his past. But he thought that he might be able to make it look better. The past was always chasing him at night, during his sleep, when it became up-front and bold, when he took a walk in the nearby park, sat under a cactus tree, read books, walked distracted in the streets, or paced up and down in the small apartment till he made Fanny dizzy.

"Can't you stop your pacing back and forth like a pendulum?"

"I'm thinking!"

"But the apartment is too small for that."

"You know, the floor space of our house in Baghdad was 600 square meters. I used to walk around as if I were in a palace, and not in a tiny apartment."

"Far from Baghdad and your mother tongue, you will always remember that you lost something, but you won't recognize that."

He was silent. Fanny wasn't surprised. She knew all too well that he wouldn't admit that he was assailed by the past, even though he was trying to free himself from it, if only in appearance. He wanted to distinguish himself from people who remained attached for no reason to their past, their culture, and even their misery and tragedies.

The small oasis of love and affection that Fanny offered him, the beauty of Brussels, and its peaceful life, couldn't make him forget his old life and his past, which loomed like a lighthouse within him. In Iraq, he had been a well-known musician. Now he was nobody. No one cared about him. He resigned himself to this fate. He liked to compare himself to a root covered with weeds that one day might break through in this place, in Brussels. He would prove to others the validity of his ideas and the meaning of his life that was fashioned by music.

Nabil always dreamed about foggy mornings in Brussels, which reminded him of the foggy mornings on the Tigris. What was different was that, when he was a child, he always feared the monstrous creature that arose out of the Tigris, spewing fire from its mouth as he had once read in *The One Thousand and One Nights*. Here, when he walked along the bank of the Meuse River leaning against the rail, contemplating the roiling waters and listening to the clamor of the city, he would remember the beautiful, dark nights on the Tigris River.

The first city was like the story of the first woman in a man's life. It might not be great, but it was difficult to forget. The first city, the first blunder, the first tremor of excitement, the first cigarette, the first glass, and the first kiss with its sweetness and warmth. Nabil remembered the vase on the table when the family gathered on summer nights; the silver platters; the crystal glasses; the shiny coffee cups; the white mousseline curtains drawn wide open; the soft light of sunset filtering into the living room; his mother's round face filling the frame of the photo; his father's and grandfather's photos on the wall; the brimful teacups in the dim light of the living room; and the Arabic books which the family had passed down from one generation to the next.

XII

Isn't there life here? Nabil was in the café listening to a song about a European girl's desire to leave Europe and emigrate because she couldn't find happiness. *Where would she emigrate?* he wondered in surprise.

Why would this girl want to leave, while he himself had moved here? Perhaps she didn't like Europe; maybe she feared a nuclear war, or a serial killer or gunfire at dark. The depression Nabil could see in European people was not justified at all. This was a sad condition—a lying refrain, a desire to escape, indifference, boredom. It was a Schopenhauerian existential and nihilistic philosophy, which was why Nabil had never liked Wagner's music. At the same time, he saw in this desire to leave a luxury, a joke, nothing serious or realistic.

"But everybody's afraid."

"Afraid of what?"

"Afraid of catastrophe!"

People have no place to hide, thought Nabil. There was no consolation to be found anywhere but in bed with a girl. After each catastrophe, people needed sex, alcohol, drugs, and sleep. In the morning began a new day.

♪

"It's weird. Even Belgian people think about fleeing and finding refuge." He took a sip from his glass and asked Fanny, perhaps sarcastically, "Why don't they go to Iraq?"

"Because they want to go to a better place," she replied.

Nabil knew very well that Fanny didn't want to hear his opinion of Belgium. She never asked him what he thought about the comedians that made fun of the country. Or how he felt about those who held pessimistic views of Belgium and saw it drowning in a political quagmire, who screamed every day, "One day there won't be a Belgium anymore!," "Do you know how shitty our political situation is?," "We're the most ignorant people in the world," or, "Don't think you live in a great country. Really, this country is nothing!" These critics were Belgian, and they were right. They were citizens. They'd been born here. *What right do I have to criticize them?* Nabil wondered.

Could he, for example, make fun of Belgian politicians? Could he despise them? Could he say, "This country is shitty?" Could he make jokes about the Walloons or the Flemish? Could he say he was miserable and afraid or that he had no rights, that this country was governed by a mafia mentality? Or were these ideas for citizens only, while he had to sit and keep quiet?

Nabil felt that in this country he was only free to talk about two things: the tragedy in his own country, and the happiness he now enjoyed here. Fanny, his intimate friend, could say that life was miserable here, but she would only smile when she heard him talk about his own happiness here—how he had been saved from his country and found peace, a place to sleep, food, and a shower.

"What if Belgium didn't exist? What would have happened to me?"

This statement was the only thing that could make Belgians feel they were Belgians. It made them feel love for their country. As for his criticisms of Belgium, they had no need of them. Even when it came to music, the only offer he got was to play with a group of amateurs on Refugee Day.

"Are you a refugee?"

"I'm a cellist!"

"But you're a refugee in Belgium."

Upset, he wanted to say, "When it comes to music, it's Belgium that's found refuge with me."

But he held back this angry retort. He felt that if you weren't from Europe, you were a refugee. You weren't supposed to be like them, and you weren't to voice your opinion. They loved it when you praised their country, but if you wanted to do what Belgians did when they expressed their hatred toward their own country and say, for example, "What a trashy place this country is!" a terrifying moment of silence would follow.

Then they would say, "You should be happy here. If you were in another country, they would have sent you back to the hell you came from."

Or they would say, "You should be grateful. Who knows what would have happened to you if we hadn't accepted you here?"

Everyone would become Belgian—not just the government, but even the taxi driver.

"Are you happy here in Belgium?" was like saying, "Are you happy here in my home?"

The taxi driver would freely curse Belgium, but only when talking to a fellow Belgian.

One day Nabil said to Fanny, "A taxi driver can curse Belgian history, politicians, fries, waffles, and even its beer and chocolate. But a refugee can't. The taxi driver expects the refugee to say, 'You don't know the value of Belgium. It's the greatest country on earth . . . Oh Belgium, what would have happened to me if you hadn't opened your arms to me?'"

So, Nabil couldn't complain about the gray weather all year round, or about fries and waffles, or even about the migraines he had developed from the gloomy weather.

♪

Nevertheless, what worried Nabil most wasn't the Belgians or what they believed or hoped for. He always felt they were right and that they were free to do what they wanted. He worried more about the immigrants. The problem of distrust in immigrant communities was nothing new. But little by little, this issue took on growing significance for him. It ballooned into a complex that was beyond resolution. He even concluded that his life in Belgium had been made hell by other immigrants, and that they were the people preventing him from reaching the Utopian City.

XIII

The idea of harmony went on buzzing around in Nabil's head. He was in Fanny's apartment explaining his idea that harmony was the essence of music. Any dissonant note among the instruments demolishes harmony, and the whole structure crumbles.

From this he went on to conclude that the presence of immigrants in Belgium was the primary cause of the loss of harmony in society because they came from a different culture. They represented a homogeneous bloc within their home societies. But when he lived amongst them back in Iraq, his presence had been out of tune there. It had demolished the harmony of their group.

"I was the only out-of-tune note. I was the voice that destroyed their harmony. Do you understand? That's why they threatened me and attacked me. Don't you see? When I left, they were better off!"

Nabil explained to Fanny how he had done well by leaving Iraq, and how when he left his country and came to Europe, he had given the harmony back there its best chance of success. As for him personally, he related better to the kind of social harmony he found in Europe.

"I find myself more in unison and more connected to this society than to where I was. I was more an alien there than I am here. I don't feel like an alien here. How do you explain that?"

Nabil concluded that for him, the presence of immigrants in Europe was something like an out-of-tune note, and that therefore, they ought to leave. Fanny was clearly annoyed by his harping on this idea.

Sensing this, he said, "Listen, I don't mean for this to be based on race. It's a cultural divide."

"I don't get it. What do you mean?" she asked as she put on her shirt without a bra underneath.

"I mean that the world is divided into two geographical places and so into two cultures. We are here; they are there. Whoever believes the way we do can come here, and whoever believes the way they do can go there. But in a culturally mixed society, there will be out-of-tune voices everywhere, and this is what causes chaos in the world."

"Oh Nabil, have you seen my panties anywhere?"

"Right there, by the bed." Fanny walked around naked, looking for her underwear as he followed her, carrying on his chatter.

"Listen, I came to the West looking for the Utopian City. This was one of al-Farabi's dreams, to implement standards for everything. Consequently, the city he wanted to create with his music would be a virtuous, Utopian City. Do you understand?"

"I'm listening!" she said as she sniffed her underwear before putting it on. "These are the dirty ones. I'm looking for my clean ones. I don't know where I put them."

She walked to the wardrobe looking for another pair of underwear. He followed her.

"Listen, isn't music subject to criteria and rules? As such, it serves as an example, an architectural, civilizational, and cultural model with all the transcendent values it entails. This is what al-Farabi was saying when he discussed Plato and Aristotle in *The Utopian City*."

Fanny put on her underwear and her pants and said to him, "You, listen to me! Go to the kitchen and eat the pizza that I put in the oven for you, and don't worry about these things. Otherwise, the pizza will burn like last time."

Then she kissed him on the cheek and rushed out.

XIV

Nabil always found an unexpected reason for his misfortunes. Fanny, who knew him better than anyone else, had asked him to change the water and the flowers in the vase and to water the plants. But he wasn't feeling good and had gone back to bed. He shut his eyes, and Fanny went back to reading. When she saw that he had fallen asleep, she put the book aside and kissed him on his feverish forehead.

She whispered, "You will feel better, my friend. You'll adjust to your new situation. You'll learn how to live in a different and diverse society. We can't all be just one color."

At that moment, he started out of his sleep. He opened his eyes and his mouth, wanting to say something, but Fanny put two fingers on his lips to calm him.

"Hush. Sleep, my darling. You'll feel better soon."

♪

It was a depressing morning. Nabil woke up feeling bitter. The physical intimacy with Fanny certainly strengthened their emotional connection, but he couldn't spend all his time in her apartment. As for making love in his apartment, it had become virtually impossible because of the Turk, his daughters, and Fanny's screams. What was he going to do? He couldn't afford another cello to continue his job as a musician. He had to come up with something else.

He had failed to find the Utopian City. He soon realized

that this concept as described by al-Farabi was a mere figment of the imagination. At the same time, he couldn't dismiss it as absurd.

Cold indifference in the face of what was happening was bad somehow, wasn't it?

The idea was more than a mere fantasy. Again, Nabil doubted his ability to influence things. He felt like a prisoner under the sway of an almost plausible dream: that of change!

He ended up taking a stroll along Chaussée de Waterloo. Walking down the broad sidewalk with his thoughts, he felt in harmony with the beautiful morning.

♪

The pulse of the street was unified and busy, announcing a long day of work and heavy traffic. He stopped by the gate to Delhaize Market. He needed a pack of cigarettes. He counted the euros in his pocket. He had enough to get a large can of beer as well.

The reflection of the light dazzled him. It was a beautiful sunny day in Brussels and the glow made its way to Flagey Square. He stared at the tramways passing in front of Café Belga. Crossing the street in the sunshine, he looked toward the shade that extended to the middle of the Square. A young African man sat there on a bench with a blond girl. His shoes shone like a pair of polished tin cans. Nabil slowly approached them. He greeted the young man, who returned the greeting. Nabil sat on a nearby bench, holding his beer in one hand and his cigarette in the other.

XV

The next day Nabil woke up late. Fanny had left early for work. He sat on the sofa, feeling exhausted. He thought about the Utopian City and the theory of harmony. He hoped Fanny would buy him a replacement cello. Then he could show his skills to Belgians, practice, think correctly, and compose the piece that he dreamed of offering to the people.

He read the note Fanny had left him on the wall: "Darling, I left you a large piece of Pizza Napolitano in the fridge. It will take a few minutes to heat in the oven. Don't forget to take the laundry basket to the laundromat. I left you the money in the drawer. Kisses, Fanny."

♪

He went to the kitchen, took the pizza out of the fridge, and placed it in the oven. He poured himself a Coke and looked for ketchup in the pantry but couldn't find it. He looked in the fridge; it wasn't there. He finally remembered leaving it on the balcony the day before, where he had eaten a hamburger.

On the balcony, he found the newspaper *Le Soir* open to a page with a headline announcing a demonstration organized by the far right in the streets of Brussels. The police also warned against a Salafi demonstration organized on the same day to counter the right-wing demonstration.

Nabil thought, *Why not take part in this demonstration?* His ideas needed to be tested and not just remain confined to

Fanny's apartment. His migration to the West had been a rational move. Didn't al-Farabi say that if a good person found himself in a corrupt city, he ought to leave it for a virtuous one? If this wasn't possible, he would merely live a bad life, in alienation. Death would be preferable. So, he had come to Europe, a virtuous place. But unfortunately, other immigrants had destroyed its virtues, transforming it into a chaotic and corrupt land. They were the mob, "the Lumpenproletariat" in Marx's terms, and the "Safala"—the riffraff—in al-Farabi's. Al-Farabi had described them as a corrupt group, prone to chaos, murder, stubbornness, and mischief that had no place in the Utopian City.

♪

Nabil decided to go to Parc Royal, where the right-wing demonstration was taking place, clamoring for immigrants to be expelled from the country. Of course, he didn't have a clear idea about right-wing ideology. He had never debated with one of its supporters or informed himself about their ideas. His friend Fanny was a leftist; she abhorred the behavior of extremists on both sides of the divide. She never harbored any hatred against immigrants. Her former boyfriend had been an African. Before that, she had been with a Turk, and she had a Moroccan boyfriend earlier.

But this time, things took a crucial turn. Nabil left his place on foot, then took the bus to join the demonstration. As he walked along the street, he stared at everything intently. He adjusted his glasses, examined things carefully. (He wore round, wire-rimmed Prada glasses like the ones worn by the maestro of the orchestra he had seen on the poster hanging in the music shop.) He believed that the purpose of this demonstration was to create a beautiful, harmonious world, free of any dissonance.

♪

He got to the demonstration. There were many yellow flags. People's faces were painted. Some had dyed their hair different colors. Some had curses and threats against immigrants tattooed on their bodies. The signs were written in medieval-style lettering. Nabil was oblivious to all this. Jubilant, he joined them lightheartedly and asked with the politeness he was known for if he could carry one of their signs.

Nabil's face was unmistakably that of an immigrant. He thought that belief alone could unite people, rather than a mythology of race, a metaphysics of color, or features. This is how he ended up in their midst.

"Boooo!" one of them cried, pointing to his face.

People looked so angry that he had no idea what was happening. He saw evil triggered in the eyes that stared at him. He was like prey surrounded by predators. The demonstrators snatched at him from all sides. Strong muscular hands, and even women, assaulted him.

What were they thinking? He had to explain to them that his color, his appearance, had nothing to do with his ideas. But these right-wingers weren't interested in listening. Things were clear-cut for them: he was the enemy.

"What brought you here to our country, you parasite?"

"We'll send all these rats back to their countries."

A woman screamed in his face, "You scum!"

She was a beautiful woman. If he had seen her the day before, Nabil would have invited her to have a beer. She had firm breasts like the ones he always liked in Belgian women, long, elegant legs, and irresistible buttocks. Yet she hit him on the head with the sign she carried that read: "Get out of our country!" Almost all the demonstrators were now gathered around him to crush him. He knew he was a dead man, but he imagined that the problem was a mere misunderstanding.

"Do you know my theory about harmony?"

But who would listen? The time for talk was past as far as they were concerned. He was closer to dying than to negotiating or explaining al-Farabi's theory on Utopia and harmony. He felt that they would certainly destroy him. All he could see was angry blond people with their mouths shouting and their eyes full of hatred and evil. He knew his death was imminent. The kicks to his chest and abdomen proved that these people were serious. But through their feet Nabil saw a group of bearded people wearing the white attire of Salafis.

The Salafis have arrived! They must have thought the right-wing demonstrators were massacring one of their followers. They had come to rescue their brother in faith as he became the prey of infidels. Was it possible that the Salafis had become angels of mercy sent to Nabil?

Everything was possible here in Europe! Nabil had only these Salafis to save him. They joined in with their sticks and knives in his defense, and they managed to rescue him.

They dragged him out of the reach of the right-wingers. He was breathless, almost a dead person. He was neither sad nor happy. He was just silent. He stared blankly without saying a word. The faces around him were smiling. Black beards, brown faces, white *dishdashas,* muscular chests, strong words coming out of their larynxes, rough voices—it all swirled around him as if he were in a film, not this improbable reality.

Hailing Nabil as their hero, the Salafis lifted him onto their shoulders and carried on with their demonstration. Nabil couldn't see out of his left eye because of a kick, but he was able to see out of his right eye when they cheered him on as the Muslim champion who had courageously dared to stand up to the right-wing demonstrators. Once the demonstration was over, they put him in a car, and took him to one of their homes on Chaussée d'Ixelles.

XVI

At the Salafi's home, Nabil lay on a couch next to a wall covered with a big black flag proclaiming *Allahu Akbar*, "God is greater." They offered him fruits and water. He really wanted a beer. All of them shook hands with him. There were three men. They looked like the group that had assaulted him back in Baghdad, hitting him and smashing his cello. Most likely they were Salafis, but they looked different from the Turk with his yellow moustache like a knotted rope.

Maybe they're of Moroccan origin? he guessed. *Yes, most likely.* They didn't utter a single word in Arabic but instead spoke impeccable French, which made him jealous. They commended him on his work for the sake of Islam. "Congratulations, brother. Your reward with God will be great."

♪

Nabil didn't say a word, but remained cautious and silent. They thought he was traumatized from the shock. But which shock: the shock of nearly being killed by right-wingers, or the shock of being rescued by the Salafis?

A few minutes later, the Salafis all went out to finish their fight with the right-wingers. Nabil's mind was completely empty. His phone rang. It was Fanny, but he didn't answer. He was exhausted. He slept an hour, then woke up. A remote control was within reach and there was a TV set in front of him. He turned on the TV and started searching for a porn channel. He smiled when he found one.

Nabil saw his attachment to porn as a way of connecting with reality. Porn was a way to live in the moment when observable fact came to be inscribed in the here and now. Sex never lost its appeal when it was direct, although it could be a source of annoyance. Even so, sex didn't have to be connected to emotions, desire, or passion. Lust could change its rhythm, its flavor, and its strength by being stripped of romantic imagination and emotions, displayed in its distinctive and exciting raw elements.

♪

Nabil spent the whole day at the Salafi's house. In the morning, he returned home. He walked down the street thinking of two things: porn, and buying a cello to continue his work on music, away from theory. He also thought about Fanny. He felt his feet taking him, as they always did, toward clothing shops. His ideas were in tune with the successive changes taking place. He realized that his experience of the previous days had reconciled him with the general outlook of life in Europe.

What did life mean to him? He wasn't sure yet. But through music, he could reach conciliation beyond the apparent contradictions in the universe. The vital venues in the city—cafés, restaurants, art museums, and galleries—had revealed to him a different meaning to life.

Differences and diversity between humans could be toned down with dim lights and wine—everyone could share one culture! Many different and contradictory sights could be unified and harmonized. He met this harmony with caution, but after a while it became more familiar to him. Behind the multiple colors, differences, and contradictions of the city lay the internal signs of life. They unfolded in an intimate and unified way, but they became manifest only through multiple material contradictions.

♪

He saw a stately funeral as he walked down Chaussée d'Ixelles. An old man lay in a coffin being transported by a hearse wrapped in velvet. There were lots of flowers and wreathes. The clothing shops were filled with shoppers because it was sale season. He walked by Zara and stopped to check the price of a black tuxedo that he might wear if he took part in a chamber music concert.

He called Fanny; she didn't answer. He passed by Porte de Namur metro station. Walking in the shadow of tall buildings, then through a traffic jam, he continued thinking. He strolled underneath a pedestrian bridge, down Chaussée de Wavre, and through narrow alleys. He went into the Filigranes bookshop, where he saw a photo of himself in the newspaper *Le Soir*, being carried on the shoulders of the Salafis. The caption under the photo read, "One of the Salafis who attacked the demonstration of the Right."

He smiled and left the bookshop. In an Internet café, he checked his email. Then he rushed across the street, even though the signal was still red. He stopped by the music shop. The spot where the cello had stood was empty. He quickly disappeared before the old salesperson could see him. He passed by vegetable kiosks on the street across from his apartment. He bought some fruit and climbed the stairs of the building. He opened a drawer in the kitchen, grabbed a knife, and peeled an orange. Then he opened the balcony and put the peels in the trashcan.

He ate the orange and decided to take a bath.

Interview with Ali Bader

Ikram Masmoudi (IM): How did you start writing *Musician in the Clouds* and what was the context you wrote it in?

Ali Bader (AB): The novel came as a reaction to the 2016 bombings in Brussels [Belgium], when ISIS-affiliated terrorists attacked the Brussels airport and Maalbek Metro station in a series of explosions. I tried to remember my first few days after I arrived in Brussels as a refugee from Iraq fleeing the Islamists and the unprecedented violence they had caused in Iraqi society. The strange thing was that I moved into an area where both Arab and Muslim immigrants lived. It felt as if I had found in Brussels the same people I had left in Iraq. They would greet anybody in the Arabic language and once you returned their greeting, they would start asking for a donation to build a mosque. So I would avoid them. I remembered this experience and wanted to write it down. At the same time, I have been interested in the concept of musical harmony, where different sounds are integrated into a complex and perfect composition. In this regard, Western music is exceptional in the way it emphasizes harmony. In any case, I am interested in and drawn to the idea of understanding the world through music.

IM: How should we situate *Musician in the Clouds* in the context of the literature of exile or migrant literature? It is a very important theme in the history of modern Arabic literature, especially now that there are many Iraqi authors writing about migration in the age of globalization.

AB: This novel is a satire on the literature of exile. Generally, this kind of writing relies on three principles: nostalgia or homesickness, suffering, and tragedy. The exiled person in the story is usually portrayed as having longings for his home country, and, at the same time, as suffering from racism and discrimination in the new society. All of this makes this kind of literature tragic in its essence. By contrast, in my novel, the main character Nabil doesn't feel nostalgic for his home country at all; he is not homesick and has no feelings of national pride or religious connection. Because of this he has more freedom in the new society he had dreamt about and mentally created through his readings in literature, cinema, and culture. In other words, it is an imagined West. At the same time, Nabil has a disdain for immigrants who distort the image he has of the West, and which he wants to be purely "Western." To him, immigrant communities destroy the harmony of his image of the West. Hence my novel, which is about migration, is a subversion of the literature of exile and a dramatic irony, where irony is a political tool to challenge existing authority.

IM: Nabil has contradictory personality traits: he is simultaneously strong and sensitive, smart and naïve, and dreamy while being aware of the reality surrounding him. Could you explain these contradictions?

AB: Yes, he lives "with his head in the clouds," as we would say in English, hence the title of the novel. He is also daring; he says things in a shocking way. His innocence and the naïveté with which he approaches the world give him more freedom to speak the truth. The truth flows from the mouths of the innocent, as in the story of the Emperor's new clothes. Nabil doesn't hide or keep anything to himself: he thinks, dreams, and speaks and does everything in front of us, as it were.

IM: While he is innocent and naïve, he makes for a powerful and independent spirit; he doesn't subscribe to common widespread ideas.

AB: Yes, and here, too, we touch upon another difference from the traditional portrayal of the exile, who is usually victimized and broken, while the West is presented as a rescuer offering him help and support. Westerners prefer victims, not strong people. The exile must play the role of the victim even if he wasn't one to start with, and the new Western society will provide him with everything. This makes the Westerner feel superior; it's a comedy! The exile cries and the Westerner wipes away his tears while continuously reminding him that he is a refugee and indebted to the West. Nabil's situation corrects all of this: when he is invited to a music show on the Day of the Refugee, he stands up to the person who reminds him that he is a refugee by telling him, "I am a cello player and when it comes to music, it is Brussels who finds refuge with me!" However, he also criticizes other immigrants.

IM: Isn't it a bit awkward and strange that he mocks and criticizes other immigrants?

AB: Nabil doesn't hate refugees or immigrants. However, he thinks through the lens of music. He believes in the concept of harmony and the possibility of curing the world's ills through musical tradition. He sees the world as out of balance, and music as a natural cure through the idea of harmony and consonance. The world can be improved through music.

Nabil tries to visualize society as an orchestra. But this is an idealistic view; it doesn't work out because there are so many instruments not playing in concert. He loses hope in the possibility of harmony, because immigrants are not ready to be integrated into the orchestra. Instead, they remain outside the orchestra and even try to disturb it. Nabil observes the behavior of some Muslim immigrants in the West, who believe they are purer than Westerners. They come carrying their culture and traditional attire with them; they think and live in the same ways they did in their countries of origin. The new society doesn't see these immigrants as alien, but paradoxically, the immigrants see the new society as alien, and they begin to change it. The relationship between the immigrants and the new society is based purely on economic gain, while Nabil disdains the economy and is uninterested in anything that is not connected to the arts. Moreover, he says all this in a shocking way and is sometimes not politically correct.

IM: Talking about the economy leads me to ask you about certain concepts you use in the novel, such as the *Lumpen*, which is a Marxist expression. By this term, do you mean to refer to the working classes? Why did you choose this concept, and how does it apply to Muslim immigrants in Belgium and in the West in general?

AB: The word *Lumpen* means worn out clothes in the German language. In Marx's theory it refers to an underclass that has nothing to do with production or productivity. It is the mob, the crowd. During Marx's time, the Lumpen could be farmers who had migrated to cities, the homeless, soldiers who had fled military service, tricksters, swindlers, pimps, etc. In his *Communist Manifesto*, Marx describes them as "the dangerous class, the social scum, that passively rotting mass thrown off by the lowest layers of old society" whose status renders them potential tools in the hands of capitalists against the working class and revolutionaries. Rosa Luxemburg calls them "the soft proletariat," and Hannah Arendt "the class drooping," referring to a corruptible class with very little consciousness of its interests. For Nabil, they are immigrant groups that live on the margins of society, who do not produce anything and who do nothing to integrate.

IM: One might argue that this class exists in all societies.

AB: Yes, and its threats depend on the space it occupies. The problem of Arab societies is the existence of a Lumpen proletariat which devours modernity. It is made up of populous crowds that are anti-modernity and anti-democracy: mafia groups, and armed militias who are easily manipulated by money and power. It also serves as a reservoir for migration to the West.

IM: This novel is a novel of ideas; it is clearly not just a plot narrating certain events, but a tool for social and cultural analysis.

AB: Absolutely! The novel for me is not just a story, but a great tool for critical analysis and understanding. It relies on and uses the methods of the social sciences as applied to a narrative context. This makes the novel closer to life than the social sciences. In fact, it surpasses them, because in the sciences there is no room for contradictions, while the novel, like life, is full of contradictions; it accommodates and even thrives on contradictions.

IM: Could you explain more? Did you study the humanities?

AB: I started my literary career with the ambition to study the humanities. At the university I was influenced by the great thinkers and philosophers of the time such as Michel Foucault, Jacques Derrida, Edward Said, and Pierre Bourdieu, among others, and I wanted to become a university professor. But I discovered that the social sciences in the Arab world and the Middle East are dead. The authorities have destroyed them, because they rely on state institutions and financing and are thus not free to say the truth. On the other hand, I found more freedom in the novel as a form of investigation and understanding. The novel is an individual pursuit. It makes a lot of room for social and cultural analysis, which is why I have suggested that the novel be an alternative to the social sciences in the Arab world. When my Western friends who want to travel to the Middle East ask me questions about the region, I tell them to go and read some novels, because novels are closer to reality than books on politics or sociology.

IM: You also talk about individuality in Nabil's relationship with his girlfriend Fanny. Do you find individuality a characteristic of Western societies?

AB: Certainly! Nabil realizes that Fanny has a strong sense of her own individuality and an attachment to her privacy, which is something he didn't think individuals could enjoy in his country. People there move as a group, while Fanny lives in harmony with the group in her society and, at the same time, enjoys her private life, which is sacred. Even though he is in a relationship with her, he cannot infiltrate her private sphere. And that's exactly the opposite of what happens in the East, where your privacy can easily be infiltrated by family, the state, or others in general—the sect, the tribe, the society. The private space is very important; it is what makes individual people different from one another. Collectivity kills creativity and distorts progress, while individuality builds individuals and helps them integrate into the group through their distinctiveness and singularity. And it is the private space that creates democracy. The failure of democracy in our countries is in large part because of the absence of the private individual. There are elections in the Middle East, but elections don't necessarily mean democracy. Voters are not free, because they are not considered individuals. They are bound to all sorts of ties and forces— familial, tribal, sectarian, and religious. What Nabil observes is this individuality, which is vital to human dignity.

IM: Nabil doesn't have a clear political perspective in terms of traditional categories. We can't tell whether he is on the left or on the right.

AB: Nabil espouses art, but rejects any political ideology. The only way for him to understand politics is to accept all contradictions, both a thesis and its antithesis. He does not focus on one position, but gives free rein to his ideas, which unfold spontaneously before the reader. Therefore, we don't find one specific voice in the novel, but a dialogue between different views. He entertains some shocking views, some anarchist ideas, as well as liberal, leftist, and right-wing notions, but he doesn't adopt one clear and definite position.

IM: How can we explain the end of the novel and the violence done to Nabil?

AB: After he is subjected to violence when his cello is destroyed in the West, he loses hope for and interest in the utopian city (an idea put forth by the Arab philosopher al-Farabi) that he had set out to search for in the Western world. The first time his cello is destroyed, he is in his own country. He assumes this won't happen to him again, especially not in the new society. But to his dismay, it does happen again, which drives a nail in the coffin of his idea of the utopian city. He had assumed that the harmony that characterizes Western music must also be a feature of Western society, but he doesn't find the harmony he had expected to in the West. One of the ideas that al-Farabi posited about the utopian city is its harmony. Those who destroy harmony prevent the utopia from materializing. Therefore, it is necessary to get rid of these dissonant elements by creating another condition for harmony—for example, by sending them off to a place where they can live together in keeping with their own values. Nabil wouldn't mind the bigots if they lived far away from him in their own kingdom. But when he goes to take part in a far-right demonstration, he realizes that, for them, it is not about values.

IM: The Western right wing has an affinity with the bigots among the immigrants.

AB: Exactly. For them, integration doesn't rely solely on shared values; they define Western identity in terms of physical appearance, color, and race, while Nabil sees it as based on values. When he gets to the demonstration, he is violently attacked simply because he doesn't look like the other demonstrators.

IM: The end of the novel is quite strange, with Nabil's desire for simple basic things. He seeks out peace and quiet, takes a shower, and eats an orange!

AB: Yes. There are three events that cause him to evolve in his ideas, and each of them prompts a violent attack on his body, while his cello is destroyed twice. The first assault is in Iraq, and it forces him out of his country. He goes to the West on a quest for harmony, as he assumes he will find it there. The second time he is assaulted is also by Muslims, but in the West, and his second cello is destroyed. He then loses faith in the existence of harmony and starts thinking that it can exist only if immigrants are kicked out. When he is assaulted a third time by right-wing protesters, he relinquishes all these complex ideas and wants to live free of any ideas. He realizes that the solution is to immerse himself in social life and enjoy life's simple pleasures. Eating the orange is a symbol of his return to a simple life, without complex thoughts. It's a return from abstraction to the sensory, if you will.

IM: Who are your favorite authors, ones that might have influenced you?

AB: I studied French literature in Baghdad, but I always liked American literature and the authors of American classics such as Jack London, Herman Melville, Steinbeck, Hemingway, Faulkner, etc. But in the 1990s, I discovered the Jewish writers of New York such as Saul Bellow, and this was a turning point for me. Reading Saul Bellow changed my ideas and my way of viewing the Iraqi person. Saddam Hussein had created an image of the Iraqi as someone who is morose, dark, unshakable, faithful, and heroic—that is, in his own image and the image of his guards, with their thick dark moustaches. I wanted to rewrite this into another kind of Iraqi: one who is shaken, whom you can laugh at and like; an Iraqi in all his humanity, foolishness, and contradictions. In his novels Saul Bellow mocks the Jewish person, while at the same time making him likable because he is humanized in all his contradictions.

IM: Do you identify as Iraqi, or Belgian, or both?

AB: I don't identify as either of these anymore. It's either about looking back to the past, or feeling more in tune with the present. I don't have any nostalgia for a city I've visited or lived in in the past, not even for my birthplace Baghdad, and I don't feel perfectly in tune with Brussels either, the city where I live now. I always long for cities I have never seen; I long for the next place I will visit and not for the one I visited last. Writing gives me freedom, and this is very important to me, as it enables me to identify as a writer; that is who I am. I don't think of my identity in religious or national terms. I am an Arab intellectual living between two worlds, East and West. Nonattachment to a particular place also gives me the freedom to take a critical stance, to distance myself and to gain in understanding. I always maintain a distance from the societies I live in; my real place is in language and writing, which enables me to criticize Arab societies rather than remaining entrenched in their culture, and to criticize the West with the same force.

IM: How do you write a novel? Do you have a ritual?

AB: When I write, I spare no effort and no time; I work like a slave for hours without breaks. I first prepare for my writing by traveling, researching, and documenting, looking for the relevant information, photos, old newspapers, etc., and I do whatever it takes to obtain the information I need, no matter how unimportant it might seem, or how long it takes me.

When it comes to the writing itself, I like to work in coffee shops, bars, restaurants, on buses, and in airports, not at home or in a quiet, remote place. I can't write in my pajamas, for example, or without wearing my shoes and my belt. I dress up in the morning and go out to write. I go to places crowded with people and events . . . it is only there—near markets, cinemas, bars, and public parks—that I can feel the pulse of the place and the warmth of the air. I can only feel the rhythm of writing in lively places amidst the smell of beer, fresh fruits, cigarette smoke, and women's perfume. It is out of this ferment that a novel is written.

About the Author and Translator

Ali Bader is a leading Iraqi novelist, essayist, poet, and screenwriter, and the winner of five major literary awards. He studied philosophy and French literature in Baghdad. He has worked as an actor, a columnist for Arabic newspapers, and a war correspondent. In his novels, Bader challenges prevailing stereotypes about his region and the ideology of extremists. He currently lives in Brussels. His novels have been translated into English, Italian, French, Dutch, and Farsi, among others.

Ikram Masmoudi is an Associate Professor of Arabic Studies at the University of Delaware. She was educated in Tunisia, France, and the United States. Her research interests include modern Arabic language and literature, translation, migration, and war fiction. She has published numerous academic articles and is the author of *War and Occupation in Iraqi Fiction* (2015); she is currently working on a book about apocalyptic imaginings in Arabic fiction.